WHITE PLUMES ASTERN

Portrait of author by Sub-Lieutenant W.H. Elliot, RCNR. (PAC C127027)

WHITE PLUMES ASTERN

THE SHORT, DARING LIFE OF CANADA'S MTB FLOTILLA

To:- Jermie of the 29th
M.T.B Flotilla
Best wishes

Tony

CDR C. ANTHONY LAW, DSC, CD, RCN (RTD)

NIMBUS PUBLISHING LIMITED

Published by:
Nimbus Publishing Limited,
P.O. Box 9301, Stn. A
Halifax, Nova Scotia
B3K 5N5

Editing and design: Heather L. Ebbs, Ontario
Cover design: Kathy Kaulbach, Halifax

Cover: *Windy Day on the Normandy Beaches*, painting by C. Anthony Law; permission to reproduce courtesy of the Art Curator, Vimy House, Ottawa

Portrait of author by Sub-Lieutenant W.H. Elliot, RCNR (Page ii)
British Power Boat Girls by Jane Shaw (Page 12)
All other drawings by C. Anthony Law

Photographs:
Pages 9, 111 and 163 courtesy of Carl Vincent
Page 145, C. Anthony Law
All other photographs appearing in this book are the property of the National Archives of Canada and have been reproduced here with permission.

Canadian Cataloguing in Publication Data

Law, C. Anthony (Charles Anthony), 1916–

White plumes astern
Includes index.
ISBN 0-921054-27-0

1. World War, 1939–1945 — Naval operations, Canadian. 2. Torpedo boats — Canada. 3. Canada. Royal Canadian Navy. History — World War, 1939–1945. I. Title.

D779.C2L38 1989 940.54'5971 C89-098583-9

Nimbus gratefully acknowledges the assistance of the Canada Council and the Nova Scotia Cultural Affairs Division.
Printed and bound in Canada

The production of *White Plumes Astern* in book form was originally undertaken by Canada's Wings Inc. of Stittsville, Ontario, whose president, Carl Vincent, had encountered the manuscript and drawings in the National Archives of Canada and recognized their merit. The design concept and historical editing were Carl Vincent's, while editing, design, typesetting and layout were done by Heather Ebbs. Unfortunately, when the book was ready to go to press, unforeseen circumstances prevented its publication by Canada's Wings Inc. However, the volume as it now stands is prepared from the material and design created and supplied by that company.

CONTENTS

PREFACE

(PAC C127042)

THIS IS THE BIOGRAPHY of the 29th Canadian Motor Torpedo Boat Flotilla. It is written with the intention of painting a picture in the minds of the readers of life in an MTB flotilla, whether it be British or American, and of sharing the happy times, as well as the sad, which the 29th experienced throughout its career in the English Channel. Mind you, there were other flotillas that did greater work—but this is the story I know best, because as the Senior Officer, I was able to watch it unfold before my eyes. I wish to take this opportunity to express my sincere appreciation and thanks to my wife, Jane, who took the whole story down in longhand as I rambled on; to Mrs. Dorothy Russell Patterson, who did the initial editing of the book and ironed it into shape; and to the late Doctor Gilbert N. Tucker, for putting in the finishing touches. I also wish to mention Doctor Fraser Nicholson for his help.

C. Anthony Law

FOREWORD

I AM DELIGHTED TO HAVE BEEN ASKED to contribute the foreword to this exciting book.

I first met Tony Law in the summer of 1942 at Dover. Both of us were commanding Torpedo Boats in the British Coastal Force, and we quickly discovered a common interest in painting. We were able to have lengthy conversations about our favourite painters and our own ambitions in the field of art when the war was over.

The flotilla of Steam Gun Boats (SGBs) which I was commanding had been fighting a fairly vigorous campaign in the English Channel, with an average, for a period, of two battles a week, either against convoys and their escorts passing through the Channel close to the French coast, or against E-Boats which came across to our coastal convoy lanes to lay mines or attack with torpedoes. For a rest I was appointed rather briefly to the Training Staff of Coastal Force at Holyhead and there met again my friend Tony Law, who had come with his 29th Canadian Motor Torpedo Boat Flotilla for a refresher course and a short working-up period. In our off-time we jointly undertook some artistic decoration of the Officers' Mess at the working-up base.

When next we met, the following year, I was Staff Officer Operations to the Captain, Coastal Force, based at Portsmouth, when Tony was commanding his MTB flotilla in some fierce fighting at the eastern end of the landing beaches in Normandy, where the German R-Boats were trying to get in to lay mines in the supply channel—the Spout, as it was called—leading into the Seine Bay and down which all the supplies were poured for the Allied invasion of Europe. Tony's contribution against the R-Boats was outstanding and earned him the highest respect in British naval circles.

We both survived those hazardous times, and in the 41 years since then, we have both been fortunate enough to have been able to pursue our peacetime profession as painters.

It is with enormous pleasure that I commend to the reader this delightful book, written and illustrated by an old friend who is also a very distinguished Canadian painter.

Sir Peter Scott, OBE, DSC, RNVR

INTRODUCTION

THE MOST CLOSELY FOUGHT ENGAGEMENTS of the Second World War included the small, highly manoeuvrable Motor Torpedo Boats (MTBs) of the Royal Navy's Coastal Force. Vulnerable to aircraft attack by day, the MTBs normally operated at night, moving through minefields into harbour defences and taking the war closer to the enemy coast. Although their main objective was to attack and destroy enemy shipping with torpedoes, taking advantage of their high speed to disengage under a smoke screen, the MTBs were employed on many other types of operations. In the Aegean and Adriatic Seas they behaved like the buccaneers of old, attacking and boarding enemy merchant ships. On other missions they would land agents on the enemy coast or transport commandos on coastal raids. All the major belligerents had boats comparable to the British MTBs. Americans had nearly identical PT boats; Germans used *Schnellboote* (or E-Boats as they were known to their opponents); Italians had their MAS boats. MTBs operated in every major theatre of the war, including the English Channel, the North Sea, the Mediterranean, Adriatic, and Aegean Seas, Burman and Malayan waters, the South China Sea, the Pacific Islands, and, toward the end of the war, the Philippines. In all their many and exciting roles the little boats were a magnificent sight, but they looked their best when planing at high speed, leaving a beautiful white plume astern.

The Coastal Force craft of the Second World War evolved from the Motor Launches (MLs) and Coastal Motor Boats (CMBs) of the First World War. The first 50 MLs were ordered by Admiralty in July 1915 from America, and proved so successful that an additional 500 were secured. The MLs were 80 feet long, with two 250-horsepower engines enabling them to travel at 20 knots. They were used extensively during the Great War for minefield sweeping, anti-submarine warfare, and escort duty, and they played a prominent part in the attempt to block the German-occupied harbours of Zeebrugge and Ostend.

In 1916, while the newly built MLs were still arriving in the United Kingdom, Admiralty accepted a design from Thornycroft for a 40-foot MTB. Twelve of these craft, known as Coastal Motor Boats, were ordered, and shortly afterward the design was modified to a 55-foot boat carrying two 18-inch torpedoes* and powered by two 375-horsepower engines, giving the boat a speed of 35 knots. The CMBs took part in many exciting operations along the Belgian coast, in the North Sea, and, after the end of the First World War, in Russian waters. The most successful of all their missions was the raid on Kronstadt harbour on the night of 17-18 August 1919, in which eight CMBs took part. The small boats torpedoed two battleships and a submarine depot ship for the loss of only three CMBs, thus altering the balance of sea power in the Baltic. This battle clearly demonstrated the value and power of a surprise torpedo boat attack on a well defended enemy harbour.

Between the two world wars MTBs had to depend upon private companies for their development. For many years Admiralty expressed no interest in small craft, mostly because of the lack of funds and lack of experience in senior staff. In the late 1930s two British companies, Vosper and British Power Boat Company, developed designs for hard-chine MTBs which, with the minimal

*These torpedoes were launched over the stern, necessitating an immediate hard turn to port or starboard by the CMB to avoid being "hoist by its own petard".

curve of their lower hull, could be more readily produced. Admiralty was once again considering smaller vessels, and fierce competition began between Vosper and British Power Boat to secure official contracts. In 1938 Vosper was awarded a contract, so British Power Boat shipped a prototype of their design to the United States to take part in an MTB design competition sponsored by the US Navy. There they met with success, and their design was used to build the US Navy's PT-9 series. A second prototype was shipped to Canada in 1939, and this design, known as the RCN CMTB 1, instigated the establishment of the Canadian Power Boat Company in Montreal.

When the Second World War broke out in 1939 the Royal Navy had 28 Coastal Force craft, 12 of which were in Malta, six in Hong Kong, and the remaining ten in the United Kingdom. In 1942 a powerfully armed MTB, known as the Fairmile 'D' boat, was developed. Built near the end of the war, this type carried a formidable armament of light guns and four torpedo tubes, which unfortunately reduced the speed to 30 or 32 knots. The Fairmile 'D', although the best of the British MTBs, was still outmatched by the German E-Boat, a heavily armed torpedo boat which could travel at 46 to 48 knots. The E-Boat was powered by a supercharged diesel engine, lessening the dangers of fire and explosion which weakened the gasoline-fuelled British MTBs.

Hundreds of MTBs built during the war years added to the size and strength of Coastal Force and contributed greatly toward a balanced naval force. By 1944 there were approximately 80 times as many officers and men in Coastal Force as in 1939. By the end of 1945, when the European War was coming to an end, 1,560 MTBs had been built. During the war Coastal Force engaged in 780 separate naval actions, 464 of which were in the English Channel and North Sea. In those 464 battles, 269 enemy ships were sunk for a loss of only 76 Coastal Force craft.

Some of the MTBs were manned by Canadians on loan to the Royal Navy. Many Canadians served with great distinction on MTBs in the English Channel and the North, Mediterranean, and Aegean Seas. A large number of Canadians were decorated for their outstanding contributions to Coastal Force—Tom Fuller of Ottawa, Bill Burke of Montreal, Corney Burke of Vancouver, and Ross Campbell of Ottawa, to name a few.

By 1937 I could see that a serious storm was gathering as Hitler became more and more aggressive. When I attempted to sign up for the Royal Canadian Navy Volunteer Reserve (RCNVR) in Quebec City, I was turned down because there were no openings, so I applied to the Army instead and was posted to

Opposite: An early Vosper-built MTB of the Royal Navy of the type that bore the brunt of the RN's Coastal Force activity in the first years of the war. (PAC PA143047)

No. 1 Ordnance Ammunition Company, Royal Canadian Ordnance Corps on 20 April 1937, as a Second Lieutenant. On 24 July 1939 I was promoted to Lieutenant, and when war broke out I became Officer Commanding No. 1 Ordnance Ammunition Company, and a Captain.

During a skiing holiday at Lake Beauport in January of 1940, I met Commander Fred Price, RCNVR, Commanding Officer of the Naval Division, Quebec City. In the course of our conversation I learned that the Navy was looking for young officers to serve on loan to the Royal Navy in MTBs. My earlier attempt to join the RCNVR having been thwarted, I answered opportunity's knock with no hesitation, asking Commander Price, "How do I get out of the Army?"

"No problem," replied the Commander. "You're in a non-combatant unit right now, so you'll be able to transfer to combatant service with no trouble."

First thing the next morning I went down to see Brigadier Trudeau, who arranged for my immediate transfer to the Navy. That same day I became an Acting Temporary Probationary Sub-Lieutenant in the RCNVR. Some things happen fast.

On 22 March 1940 I was appointed to HMCS *Stadacona,* where I was to cool my heels for a while with 24 other young, keen, potential officers from all over Canada. We embarked on *Duchess of Athlone* a few days later, the first group of RCNVR officers to be sent on loan to the Royal Navy, and the envy of all other young naval officers in HMCS *Stadacona* and the Canadian fleet.

Since we were unescorted, the Captain of *Duchess of Athlone* requested that we assist him by doing watches on the bridge. Keen though inexperienced, we were anxious to help, and it was perhaps fortunate that we had an uneventful crossing. We arrived at Liverpool under a grey and overcast sky, and disembarked the ship only to be then loaded onto a train. A long train ride, with a transfer at London, brought us finally to Hove. It was evening, and the blacked-out city was strange and somehow oppressive to our Canadian eyes. But with little time for heavy thoughts we were transported to our digs and then taken to the HMS *King Alfred* for a welcome meal. Captain Pelly, RN, Commanding Officer of the Officer Training Establishment at *King Alfred,* greeted us warmly, delighted with the arrival of the first RCNVR officers for training. We were all equally enthusiastic, but with the meal, speeches, and welcoming over, we took gratefully to our beds.

Beginning the next morning, we quickly became acquainted with the training base, and soon were hard at it learning how to become officers. Week-

Opposite: The Royal Canadian Navy's first Motor Torpedo Boat and the ancestor of the 29th MTB Flotilla's craft. In the background are ex-US destroyers. (RCN neg. no. 1751) ends spent in London were high points of excitement to us new arrivals; the war did not yet appear serious. The picture changed rapidly after Dunkirk. Our studies took on a new urgency, and the shadow of danger loomed before us as we completed our basic training. I went on to a special course in celestial navigation for MTBs, and in a frighteningly short time I found myself in active service aboard HMS *Wolfe.* Once known as the Canadian Pacific Steamship *Montcalm,* she had been converted into an armed merchant cruiser and filled with empty oil drums in the hope that she would sink slowly and upright if she were mortally wounded by a German raider. *Wolfe* patrolled the Denmark Straits around Iceland, sometimes running as far north as the ice-pack. Arthur Stairs, one of my fellow RCNVR officers, and I went on two or three patrols in *Wolfe* before being appointed to HMS *Osprey,* Portland, Dorset for anti-submarine training. Then on 8 March 1941 Arthur and I were appointed to a Motor Gun Boat (MGB) flotilla, I to MGB *53* as First Lieutenant and navigator. Built by British Power Boat Company and powered with Rolls Royce Merlin

engines, these boats could give tremendous speed. Unfortunately, the gear-box tended to over-heat, causing a number of problems. I did not see much action in those days, but we did experience some devastating German bombing raids, the beginning of the Battle of Britain.

The Battle of Britain presented a new difficulty for us. The heavy demand on fighters and bombers meant that the Royal Air Force had priority for all Rolls Royce engines. Until substitute engines could be supplied, many MTBs were coming off the slips with no powerplant, a severe blow to the building programme. The Packard company in the United States began to re-design the carburetor and gear-box of their engine, making several other changes as well to improve the engine for marine use. In the meantime, as an interim measure, Packard provided the Hall-Scott engine. Designed for the Fairmiles, this 600-horsepower engine was given a supercharger for its new task, boosting the power to 960 horsepower. Nonetheless, the MTBs' speed was reduced to 29 knots; the German E-Boat was doing 40 knots or better. Eventually the modified Packard engine began to arrive at British Power Boats, and the speed of the Shorts went back to the 40-knot range. After an MTB command course I was appointed Commanding Officer of MTB *48.* My first command. I was tremendously proud of MTB *48.* Built by Samuel-White at Cowes, Isle of Wight, she was engined with three Hall-Scott engines and had a speed of 29 knots, so she was no racehorse. But she was mine, all the same.

I sailed to my operations base at HMS *Wasp,* Felixstowe after work-ups at HMS *Hornet,* Gosport. At Felixstowe, MTB *48* and I joined the flotilla led by Hillary Gamble, DSC, RN. Initially we patrolled the Dutch and Belgian coastline, but it wasn't long before the flotilla was ordered to sail to "Hell's Corner" —Dover. It was at Dover that MTB *48* met the enemy for the first time. In a brief encounter with a group of German R-Boats, our boat was shot up and the motor mechanic was wounded. We had been blooded . . . and the next phase was about to begin.

On 12 February 1942, the German battle cruisers *Scharnhorst* and *Gneisenau,* accompanied by the cruiser *Prinz Eugen,* six Narvik class destroyers, and 24 E-Boats, as well as a heavy umbrella of escorting aircraft, began to approach the English Channel at the Strait of Dover. On that same day, five little Motor Torpedo Boats sailed out of Dover harbour to attack this impressive force. Our Senior Officer, Lieutenant-Commander Nigel Pumphrey, DSO, DSC, RN, led our tiny group in MTB *221;* Mark Arnold Foster was in *219;* Hillary Gamble had *45;* Dick Sunder, the Australian, was in *44;* and I had MTB *48.*

The Channel waters were roughened by a heavy wind from the south-west. Our first sight of the German force was a group of several *Messerschmitts,* high in the distant sky. As we sailed closer, a large, long smokescreen came into view. Behind it lay our three main targets. The wind gradually swirled the smoke away, and the powerful German naval force was revealed. Losing no time, Nigel began to organize us for an attack, but suddenly one of his engines died, and we were ordered to act independently.

It was an impossible situation. The 24 E-Boats kept close station, preventing any attempt to break through the screen. We were forced to fire our torpedoes from about 4,000 yards or more, a far from ideal range for Torpedo Boats. But there was nothing for it but to try, so we fired away gamely, loosing the torpedoes from all five boats. One of the battleships turned to avoid our torpedoes, but there were no hits. Suddenly one of the Narvik class destroyers appeared on MTB *48's* beam. (I later learned it was *Friedrich Ihn,* commanded by Lieutenant-Commander Wachsmuth.) Our gunner started firing, and we watched for the opportunity to release our pre-set depth charges. The destroyer was firing away with her 4.7 guns, but we were too close and too small for her, and the shells whistled overhead to find a mark somewhere beyond us. So far, luck had been on our side.

I was steering straight for Goodwin Sands, despite a warning of the danger by my First Lieutenant, for I believed that *Friedrich Ihn* would run aground first. But Lieutenant-Commander Wachsmuth turned her away to rejoin the other battleships, and the German Battle Squadron sped away through the Strait at 30 knots, gradually outdistancing our MTBs. Nigel Pumphrey was certain we would have made a better showing had we had adequate gun boat and fighter support. We had been fortunate in one respect, for the escorting German aircraft had made no attempt to attack us; perhaps they had been saving their fire for the RAF.

We were preparing to give up the chase when my coxswain touched me on the shoulder. He pointed to six approaching aircraft: "Sir, aircraft with two wings—they must be British!" It was Lieutenant-Commander Esmonde, gallantly leading his six *Swordfish* into an almost suicidal attack. They had lost their fighter escort *en route,* but bravely pressed on in their attempt to stop *Scharnhorst* and *Gneisenau.* They dropped their torpedoes, and in retaliation all six were shot down. Of the eighteen aircrew, there were five survivors.

After a number of engagements in the English Channel in MTB *48,* I was given 60 days foreign service leave during the summer of 1942. I returned to Canada, and during leave I married Jane Brumm Shaw. We had met five years earlier when she was an art student at the Ecole des Beaux Arts in Quebec City. After the wedding we spent a wonderful honeymoon in the Laurentian Mountains north of Montreal. Leave came to an end far too soon, and I returned to the UK in the autumn of 1942 to take command of MTB *629.*

MTB *629* was one of the new 'D' class Torpedo Boats, with heavy armament and four Packard engines. She was built and commissioned in Talbot, Scotland, and from there I sailed her to Weymouth for her work-ups. On completion of our training we sailed to Yarmouth to join the flotilla at HMS *Bee.* From that time until the end of 1943, one year, we operated in the North Sea off the Dutch coast, and MTB *629* and I saw much action together.

Until 1943 the Canadian Navy's major role in the Battle of the Atlantic had been played with corvettes and frigates, but by this time it had added many other ships and craft to the naval force. Its total force consisted of hundreds of corvettes and frigates, 28 destroyers, many minesweepers and landing craft, three armed merchant cruisers, two other cruisers, and one aircraft carrier, HMS *Nabob.* In 1943 the RCN began to explore the possibility of forming two MTB flotillas to add to its force.

In January 1944, Lieutenant J.R.H. Kirkpatrick, DSC, RCNVR, and I were appointed for staff duty with the Senior Canadian Naval Mission Overseas (London) in connection with Canadian Coastal Forces. Kirk and I were assigned the task of forming the two new Canadian MTB flotillas. Freddie Southam, who was also on staff at the time, helped us enormously. After studying the various available MTBs, it was decided that Kirkpatrick would form the 65th Canadian Motor Torpedo Boat Flotilla with eight 'D' class Fairmile MTBs. These MTBs were powered by four Packard engines, and with four torpedo tubes and adequate armament they were able to operate as Motor Gun Boats. At a later date two more MTBs were added to Kirkpatrick's flotilla.

I was assigned to lead the eight short boats known as the 29th Canadian Motor Torpedo Boat Flotilla. Most of the Commanding Officers of our two flotillas had gained MTB experience over the preceding years of war from their service on loan to the Royal Navy, but the other officers and men came fresh-faced from Canada.

Up to this point the RCN's role had been primarily that of escort to the many convoys to the UK, thus helping to maintain that important life-line. Now, the RCN's expanded fleet was able to take part in other naval operations, making a significant contribution to Allied sea power. The RCN was ready to take full part in the final phase of the war, and in the invasion of Normandy.

Opposite: British Power Boat girls. (Drawing by Jane Shaw, the author's wife. PAC C127043)

CHAPTER ONE

COMMISSIONING

THE YEAR WAS 1944, a year that will go down in world history because it marked the beginning of the end of the Nazi war machine. After years of a shivering fear which had crystallized into never-to-be-forgotten superhuman courage, the British people were ready to make their supreme effort to defeat the enemy on the continent of Europe, but they could not make it unaided. Five years of relentless warfare had taken their toll of British manpower. It was then, influenced by that spirit of co-operation of the Allies which was eventually to bring the hard-won victory, that the Royal Canadian Navy commissioned two flotillas of Motor Torpedo Boats—the 65th and the 29th.

The boats of the 29th MTB Flotilla were 71½-foot hard-chine craft, built by British Power Boats. Originally designed as Motor Gun Boats (MGBs), they were redesignated Motor Torpedo Boats but could be used in either role, an example of the increased flexibility in Coastal Force craft as the war ground on. The MTBs had a maximum speed of 41 knots and would start planing at 20 knots. Their armament consisted of two 18-inch torpedoes, one power-mounted two-pounder pom-pom gun forward (this was later replaced by a six-pounder power-driven gun, giving the boats much increased firepower), a twin 20-mm Oerlikon hand-operated mounting aft, and twin Vickers .303 machine-guns mounted on port and starboard, as were the two torpedo tubes and two depth charges. The engines consisted of three American Packard-built Rolls Royce Merlins of 1,250 horsepower (later replaced by 1,500-horsepower engines) and a Ford auxiliary, which generated sufficient power to run the radar and electric heating and to take care of the cooking and lighting. The vessels were equipped with smoke apparatus, the most modern radar, wireless telegraphy equipment, and the latest Admiralty fittings. The armour-plated bridge was extremely well designed for practical use, and the chart room was fitted with all the most

modern devices, including an echo-sounding machine, View Plot, and other wonders to ensure streamlined navigation. The complement required to man this type of boat was two officers and 15 ratings, but the Senior Officer's vessel carried an extra officer and signalman.

In the 65th Flotilla the boats were quite different. Known as 'D' class Fairmiles, they had been contracted by Fairmile throughout the yacht-building yards in England and Scotland. They measured 115 feet in length, and were powered by four 1,250-horsepower Packard engines, giving them a speed ranging from 29 to 31 knots, and had two Ford auxiliary engines to provide electric power. The handicap of low speed was compensated by a heavy armament. Armed with four 18-inch torpedoes, two six-pounders, two twin .5-inch power-mounted guns, twin Oerlikons, and twin Vickers hand-operated machine-guns mounted on either side of the bridge, they were nasty flak-ships. In addition, they carried two depth charges, and the bridge was armour-plated and fitted with electrical equipment similar to that in the 29th Flotilla boats. They possessed a much greater range than other MTBs, and could remain at sea in more severe weather. The Fairmile 'D' MTBs were known as "Long Boats" or "Longs" to distinguish them from the bulk of the other MTBs. These, including the 29th Flotilla's craft, were about 70 feet long (depending on the individual design) and were hence known as "Short Boats" or "Shorts". The Fairmile 'D' Boats carried three officers–Commanding Officer, First Lieutenant, and Navigating Officer–and 26 men.

The routine followed in the two flotillas was very similar to that of destroyers, though on a much smaller scale. Both types of boat proved most successful in Channel warfare, as well as in the Mediterranean, and they and their predecessors won high distinction by keeping the German E-Boats on the defensive and thus forcing the enemy to escort their own convoys. This was a major victory, because if the *Schnellboote* had operated offensively throughout the war, there would have been a far greater loss of British tonnage in the Channel. As it was, except for the dark days of 1940 and 1941, the E-Boats could make only half-hearted attempts at offensive action.

One must bear in mind that the tiny torpedo boat, at which most "big-ship" men turn up their noses, was capable of sinking a battleship with a single well placed torpedo. (Lieutenant-Commander D.G. Bradford, DSO, DSC and Two Bars, RNR, sank the 17,000-ton liner *Strasbourg* off Ijmuiden harbour, while the large and modern cruiser HMS *Manchester* was torpedoed and sunk by a pair of Italian MAS boats off Tunisia in August 1942.) Moreover, it is an

Opposite: The initial main gun armament of the 29th Flotilla's MTBs was the two-pounder pom pom, an automatic power-mounted weapon firing an approximately 40-mm shell. (PAC PA143046)

established fact that every Allied MTB or PT Flotilla in the Second World War paid for itself many times over by sinking thousands of tons of enemy merchant shipping, as well as by eliminating warships. In the early days Admiralty officials were sceptical of the value of this new branch of the Service, but as the war unfolded the boats proved themselves time and again; toward the latter part of the conflict Admiralty could not build enough of these deadly craft with the devastating sting. During the day, aircraft dealt with enemy shipping; MGBs, MTBs, and the few Steam Gun Boats (SGBs) operated only by night, when they prowled the German convoy routes seeking their quarry. The boats of the Coastal Force found it prudent not to venture forth in the daylight hours, when they would prove dangerously vulnerable to enemy air attack, chiefly because of the hundred-octane gasoline with which they were fuelled. This highly volatile fuel, demanded by the engines which had been originally designed for aircraft, was a great source of worry to Coastal Force bases throughout the war, and a number of fatal accidents did occur. This was one worry spared our opponents, whose E-Boats were diesel-powered and hence maddeningly (from our viewpoint) difficult to ignite.

The crews of MTBs had a far from easy life. The crashing rise and fall of the boats in heavy weather was often the cause of serious stomach disorders, not to mention the occasional broken bone, and in general a severe strain was imposed upon the physical and nervous systems. This was particularly true for engine-room personnel, who had to wear ear-plugs to deaden the noise of the supercharger, and whose health was constantly endangered by the gas fumes. The crews of the Short Boats usually lived ashore, but on those many occasions when accommodation was not available, they slept on board—and the congested quarters and sweating decks were anything but conducive to a healthy existence. Even in the long MTBs where the crews lived on board, accommodation was far from ideal; but in spite of these obstacles, they carried out their duties with a spirited zeal.

On 15 February 1944, I was standing on the pier at Southampton waiting for the ferry that would take me to Hythe. Overhead, fat barrage balloons shimmered in the sunshine, and gulls screamed raucously in the cold morning air. To my left, as I leaned against the wall, a large Landing Ship (LST) was gorging itself with tanks, trucks, and other choice morsels of equipment, like a whale swallowing schools of fish. Landing craft by the hundreds plied their busy way up and down the congested harbour. Eventually, the rotund little Hythe ferry emerged from this conglomeration and manoeuvred alongside the pier. I could see the old Captain ringing telegraphs to the engine room, and then with a resounding crash the ferry was docked. The Captain stepped out of the wheelhouse. He was a stereotype from a boy's pirate novel, with his

(PAC C127030)

wooden leg clumping noisily on the deck as he walked over to peer cautiously over the side with his one good eye to see if there was anything left on his ferry. When the panic and confusion of the debarking throng was over, I made my way aboard the vessel.

Once the last of the human cargo had been stowed away, the Captain, apparently satisfied that his vessel was still intact, climbed back into the wheel-house. After many engine manoeuvres he finally turned her about, and we set off across the Southampton River at the breathtaking speed of six knots. Eventually, with the usual resounding clatter, we came alongside Hythe Pier. At the top of the pier I boarded a comical little "Toonerville trolley", and for the sum of one penny was transported, none too comfortably, to the gates of the village of Hythe a half-mile away. Once again I was on familiar ground, because here, in 1940, I had commissioned MGB *53* as First Lieutenant.

(PAC C127048)

I made my way briskly toward British Power Boat Company (known to us, for the sake of convenience, simply as BP) and, after wrestling with the usual red tape of signed and countersigned passes, I was permitted to enter. After walking through the factory, I arrived at the office of Lieutenant Eric Hill, RNVR, the Admiralty representative at BP. Hill did everything for us except build the boats. We wanted charts and he got them; we wanted ammunition, he got it. He also managed to procure a goodly share of duty-free spirits. To us, he was Santa Claus. He was glad to see me, and for some time we reminisced and exchanged news on the Coastal Force types and their activities. Hill then informed me of the misfortunes that had befallen MTB *459*, my ship. The torpedo-tube trials had failed, as well as the speed trials, and she had the turning circle of the *Queen Mary.* The outlook was bleak, but like all other MTB types, I was used to that. Hill assured me that all the great brains were busy redesigning propellers and rudders. Perhaps in a week or two there would be a new trial.

The unexpected interlude gave me the opportunity to study the equipment and set-up in BP, and also the pleasure of investigating Southampton's high spots. The Chrysanthemum Club, known to us as the Honky Tonk, was *the* high spot, and it saw the beginning and ending of many a gay party.

British Power Boats, Scott Paine's fascinating factory, once housed in several small buildings, had mushroomed into a great organization. An air of crisp efficiency prevailed both in the yard and in the white-walled offices, where black floors mirrored gleaming ceilings. In the factory, carpenter girls wore cool green smocks, the clean-up girls vied for attention in bright blue, and engineers were highlighted in white. The place was a veritable rainbow of colour. I'll never forget a certain charming grey-haired lady who had been one of the carpenter "girls" (sixty, if she was a day). She had started in the workshop, sawing, drilling, and hammering the hulls into place, and she loved every minute of it, chiefly because it seemed to her that it was work toward victory. She was not only cultured and intelligent, but also, I was astonished to learn, had the private means that could have bought British Power Boats with the stroke of a pen. Eventually, she was promoted to an office position more suited to her years and dignity. Her disappointment was profound; she spent her days counting up little figures which didn't amuse her, and no longer could she wear her natty green overalls and kerchief.

The busy hum in the factory was interrupted at intervals by a soft feminine voice with an Oxford accent—whose owner was known as the Bombshell Blonde—deceptively purring urgent messages over the loudspeaker system. Then the hailer would be switched back to the BBC for "Music While You Work", the banging of hammers and buzzing of drills providing a more-than-adequate percussion section. But even this symphony was frequently drowned out by the

"Carpenter girls in cool green overalls" at British Power Boats. The boats were built upside down. (PAC C127032)

roar of engines, growing louder, then fading into the distance, as a new Torpedo Boat roared over the measured mile attempting new speed records on its Admiralty trials and acceptance.

Two weeks later the time had come to ask the Royal Canadian Navy Personnel Officer in London (Lieutenant-Commander Freddie Southam) to send for my First Lieutenant to join *459*. In a few days John Shand arrived and reported. He was a tall character, blunt and precise, with a rough manner of speech which never wasted a word, but he had the looks to make the feminine heart do somersaults. We looked over our new ship together. John was impressed with the streamlined shape, but bewildered by the millions of gadgets—radar, interrogators, and many other wonders. Mind you, I was equally perplexed, but as the Senior Officer of the flotilla, I had to look wise.

Next to appear was Jack Foote, the third officer, a short, likeable chap who seemed to spend most of his time locating and hoarding "Duty Free" for the commissioning day. Shand called him "Footsie" while all was going well, but when Jack fell out of favour, it was "Son". Footsie would get no further than "Mares eat oats and does eat oats . . . " in his favourite song before the towering Shand would glare down and snap, "That will be enough, Son!" Poor Footsie! He did a great job and was liked by all.

From then on the officers arrived in a steady stream. Lieutenant Dave Killam, DSC, and his First Lieutenant, Howard (Howie) Hunt, came next. Dave was an old veteran of Coastal Force, and having won distinction in the past, he was destined to be an important vertebra in the backbone of the flotilla. Little Howie had just come over from Canada to join us, and he was probably the shortest member. But Howie required the longest smoke; only the best of cigars would do.

To the ever-growing group was added the Divisional Leader, "Daddy Bones"—Lieutenant C.A. Burk, DSC—and Scobie, his First Lieutenant. Bones's head was thinly upholstered, which he explained with, "Green grass never grows on a busy corner." His long conversations with the dice had so impressed the English lads in the Naval Mess at HMS *Mantis* (Lowestoft), that they had christened him "Bones". While at Lowestoft he married an English nurse, and after the birth of their daughter he was additionally tagged with "Daddy"—hence "Daddy Bones"—and it stuck with him throughout his naval career. Bones was an efficient, enthusiastic officer who stayed cheerful and smiling no matter how black the outlook. Scobie, his Number One, a dark, stocky chap, had an incredible knack with cards. Whenever a little game of chance came up he excelled—the cards never seemed to fail him.

462, 463, 464, 465, and *466* were still to be commissioned, but the respective COs came for a visit from time to time. Bobby Moyse commanded *462* and Jessman was his Number One; Glen Creba, with Dick Paddon from

"Daddy Bones"
Lieutenant C.A. Burk
DSC and Two Bars
RCNVR
(PAC C104920)

Labrador, was in charge of *463;* Craig Bishop and his First Lieutenant, Joe Adams, were responsible for *464;* while Charley Chaffey commanded *465* with Vern Barlow as his Number One. And last, but far from least, was Barney Marshall, CO of *466,* and his First Lieutenant, Joe Bampton.

John Shand walked up to me one day on the British Power Boats pier and said he had just met the grandest old man, an ex-Commander in the Royal Navy, aged 72, suntanned and with the physique of an ox. He was working as a deck-hand in BP, loading hundred-pound pieces of pig-iron aboard the various MTBs for trials. His vigour and vitality put the younger ones in the shade. John was anxious that I should meet him, so we made our way to the end of the pier where this marvellous character was working, looking more like an athlete than a man of 72. Yet his appearance was typical of an old sea-dog. He had a brush cut, his sharp eyes twinkled beneath a pair of bushy brows, and he was dressed in grey flannels and a matelot's blue sweater. We were embarrassed no end because he kept calling us both "Sir" as he recounted the trials and tribulations he had encountered while trying to get back into the Service, which refused to take him on account of his age. John and I got to know him well. Every day we would stop by for a chat, and we greatly enjoyed listening to the interesting and amusing stories culled from his vast experience.

Toward the end of March, after depressing weeks of torpedo failures and speed trial failures, came the great day of the Admiralty acceptance trial. On the morning of *the* day, one person stood out from all the rest. He was a grey-haired fellow named Leonard Tilbury, who had charge of the four-hour trial. In his navy-blue suit with black buttons, crisp white shirt, and black tie, topped off with a natty yachting cap, he might have stepped straight from a page in *Esquire.* Leonard was very busy trundling back and forth from the jetty to the boat, carrying heavy boxes of hot coffee, sandwiches, beer, gin, and whiskey . . . and cigars in case the trial went well. Then, after making sure that all the Admiralty overseers, officials, and BP representatives were on board, he gave the order to cast off. MTB *459's* first and second trials had ended with damaged propellers because the measured mile had been full of flotsam. Now, on her third trial, there was only one poor point—the engine boost was a half pound too much. This greatly worried the Admiralty overseers, but not the rest of us. Four hours passed, and the Admiralty overseers grudgingly accepted her. Everyone was happy, above all little Leonard. At this point, he was offering cigars to all.

MTB 459, the author's boat and first of the 29th Flotilla to commission. (PAC PA107899)

The crew of MTB 459 on commissioning day. (C.A. Law)

In late March 1944, three days after trials, MTB *459* was commissioned, the first boat of the 29th Canadian MTB Flotilla to begin her career. A reception was given for BP's staff, and even for the Admiralty overseers. All day loads of ammunition and stores were brought aboard—it was like Christmas with all the lovely new equipment—and Lieutenant Hill assisted in his usual role of Santa Claus, while different departments of BP were busy making "rabbits" (gifts for the boats) for us. With many thanks, we finally departed from British Power Boats and sailed around to Portsmouth, up to Haslar Creek, and made fast alongside HMS *Hornet,* the Coastal Force manning base.

The commissioning of MTB 464 at British Power Boats, Hythe. (PAC C127041)

CHAPTER TWO

WORKING UP

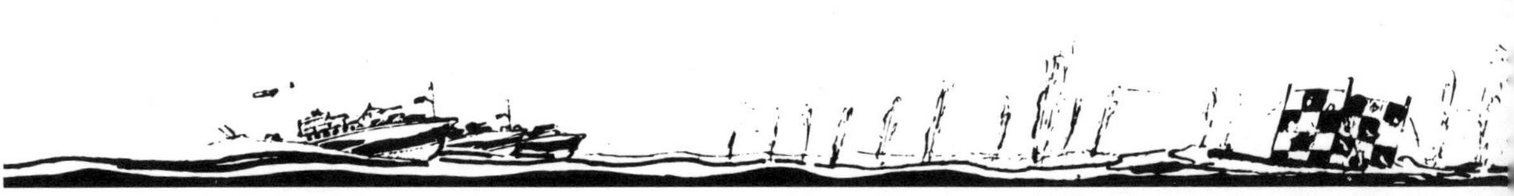

FOUR DAYS LATER MTB *459* set sail for HMS *Bee* (the working-up base for Coastal Force) at Holyhead. She was happy—happy to get away from *Hornet.* Day after day hundreds of base staff had thundered aboard and tramped back and forth over her new decks, checking the equipment and making necessary adjustments. Now, at last, she was free of these irksome strangers and content to listen to the patter of her crew's familiar footsteps.

She was falling into her stride. It was a marvellous day. There was a bit of a chop with a fresh southerly breeze, and sunlight sparkled on the roughened waters. The boat bumped down the Channel to Falmouth, leaving the Needles at the southern end of the Isle of Wight gleaming in the sun like white sculpture against a blue back-drop. We passed Portland Bill, and soon the Eddystone lighthouse loomed out of the water, warning us of the dangerous rocks beneath.

MTB *459* soon found herself entering a strange harbour—Falmouth, on the south coast of Cornwall, the home of the late renowned Lieutenant-Commander R.P. Hitchens, DSO and Bar, DSC and Two Bars, who had won such great distinction in gun boat warfare. He was the Nelson of Coastal Force.

We secured alongside, fuelled, and made all the necessary arrangements to set sail the next day; but the sailing was cancelled due to strong southerly winds. So, in the afternoon, we got permission to proceed downstream from the base into the inner harbour, where we tied up alongside an American landing craft. Immediately the Signalman was sent over, and boarding the craft

Opposite: Gun shoot at Holyhead. (PAC C127046) *Above: (PAC C127035)*

he saluted smartly and said, "With the compliments of the Captain of *459,* Sir. Request you, Sir, and your officers come aboard for a gin." Shortly afterward there was a knock on the wardroom door and in walked three pleasant-faced American officers. We soon discovered that the CO of the landing craft had been holding out on us—it was his birthday. By way of celebration the officers of *459's* wardroom presented the American Captain with a suitable gift for the occasion, one bottle of *Haig & Haig* and one of *Plymouth* gin. Our hospitality was returned by means of a great meal of large, juicy steaks, something we hadn't seen for years.

Next day we sailed out of Falmouth harbour with three hangovers on board. We were feeling extremely delicate, but had little chance to pamper our condition. Rounding Land's End we came into a strong wind (force 4 to 5), which bounced our small craft about on the waves with a rattle and crash. It was *459's* first experience of rough weather. After many hours of sailing in deteriorating weather and mountainous seas, the deck was streaming with water, officers and crew were soaked; everything was sodden. Eventually and with some difficulty we found shelter in the cosy harbour of Appledore, and there we spent the night. The following morning was glorious. *459* skimmed out over the glass-like sea, leaving Appledore harbour to mingle with the rocky landscape of the Cornish coast. Gliding through the water at the refreshing speed of 25 knots, we roared past the Isle of Lundy and Milford Haven, and in a few hours reduced speed and slowly made our way into the Welsh harbour of Holyhead.

MTB 459 during the working-up period at Holyhead. (PAC PA144586)

Holyhead is on a peninsula. To westward is a large hill which drops sharply into the green waters. Northward, extending out as far as the eye can see into the bay, a breakwater forms the sheltered harbour. The coast is rocky with jagged reefs and the waters are dotted with islets. During the winter months, stormy gales blowing for days on end whip the seas into a frenzy, making training for MTBs impossible at times.

The formidable Welsh coast is dotted with ancient ruins—monasteries, castles, and small towers placed at strategic points. In bygone days these towers were used as lookouts. The story is that from time to time, Irish warriors would raid the coast, setting fire to small towns, terrorizing the populace, and making away with spoils of feminine charm. And according to the old characters who have lived their lives in Holyhead, the Welsh did likewise on the Irish coast. But those days have long since passed, and today Holyhead is a quiet, sleepy, little town, content with its own small world. The inhabitants cling to their own language, using it in preference to English. Wales itself seems more like some small European country than a part of the United Kingdom. But even in Holyhead there was one note of suspected intrigue, supplied by the ferry which plied its way regularly to Dublin and back. It was believed that many sinister types used this rather fast coal-burning ship as a means to furthering their espionage activities. Astern of this ferry lay the MTBs.

MTB *459* made her way up toward the end of the harbour, slowly turned 180°, and made fast alongside a Free French MTB. British, Norwegian, and Canadian MTBs were also there working up. I made my way through HMS *Bee* toward the operations room, and thence to the training office to pay my respects to the base Captain, Captain the Honourable E. Pleybell-Bouverie, RN. After a long discussion with many of my Coastal Force friends, including Lieutenant-Commander Peter Scott, OBE, DSC, RNVR,* I returned to the docks and boarded Lieutenant-Commander Kirkpatrick's boat, *748*. Old Kirk, more familiarly known as "The Brain", was the Senior Officer of the 65th Canadian MTB Flotilla, and was a tall, thin chap with a protruding forehead and blue eyes that somehow reminded one of a St. Bernard. He gave me a brief outline of what I might expect. One problem was trying to get Canadian sailors into the rig of the day. These free spirits had proved to be rampant individualists in the matter of dress and had no intention of yielding to conformity in this regard, despite any sternly worded instructions. It was a losing battle, which sometimes overshadowed the war itself.

**The only son of Captain Robert Scott of Antarctic fame, Sir Peter Scott, OBE, DSC, RNVR, who contributed the foreword to this book, has achieved personal fame as an explorer, naturalist, and sportsman. This world-renowned conservationist is perhaps best known for his wildlife art. During the Second World War he served with distinction in the Royal Navy and Coastal Force, making major contributions to the art of camouflage.*

Before dinner a rollicking party commenced in the Mess. The representatives of the various Allied nations, propped around the bar, were in high spirits. The rounds of beer came by so fast that our back teeth were soon floating, and the Mess resounded with laughter, naughty stories, and risque songs. There was a spherical gentleman—one Basil Ward (Lieutenant, DSC and Bar)— who had a particular capacity for inventing anything conducive to fun. His sense of humour was unsurpassed, and we were kept constantly amused with his witty stories. He was well loved for his cheerfulness and greatly respected for his fighting ability, for he had gained distinction in his many battles in the Strait of Dover. During the evening Peter Scott and I had a long conversation on the subject of art. We both loved to paint, and did so whenever we could get the chance. He and I had decorated the Wardroom Mess of HMS *Bee.* Much too soon the bar closed and the party was at an end. Laughter, songs, natter—they no longer echoed in the room; the quiet was guarded by the wild geese in Peter's mural, and the base settled softly to sleep.

The next morning dawned crisp and clear, and the air was nippy as we went out for our semaphore and flashing exercises. I could hardly see anything that early in the morning, and was very rusty at my signals in any case. Only the odd "A" and "B" or long break was recognizable. The lesson ended with dispersal to our boats, and I was proud to have my crew in spotless white sweaters ready for our first lecture by the training commander. He expressed his pleasure in having us and hoped the working-up period would be pleasant and of value to us. He then outlined our organization and training programme. Soon the 29th was hard at work, and we greatly enjoyed our new and varied activities. Mornings brought lectures on various subjects, and in the afternoons we went to sea for torpedo exercise. This consisted of a few dummy runs on the target ship and then the firing of a torpedo with a blowing head. Our instructor for these exercises was Warrant Officer Church, affectionately known as "Curly" because he hadn't a vestige of hair. He was the very essence of enthusiasm, and we were quickly infected with his keenness. We all began to play our parts as if we were in a real action.

After we dropped W/O Church off in harbour, Lieutenant Smith, the radar "king", came aboard. "Smithie" was a great fellow, with a commendable aptitude for getting the radar ratings, navigators, and Commanding Officers working together as an efficient team. I would sit on the floor of my bridge, the navigator's chart room windows would be blacked out, and the exercise would start, with Smithie keeping a sharp look-out to avoid collisions and at the same time checking the ability of the radar operator in picking up the

Opposite: MTB 459 during the working-up period at Holyhead. (PAC PA144589)

459
459

target, which was another MTB acting as a German E-Boat. The conversation between the bridge, the navigator, and the radar operator would run something like this:

Radar Operator: 291 Bridge.

CO: Bridge 291.

Radar Operator: Echo bearing, red one-zero, range three-five-zero-zero yards, amplitude 1x.

CO: Watch and carry out all-round sweep.

CO to Navigator: Plot bridge.

Navigator: Bridge plot.

CO: Start plotting the enemy, and get course and speed.

After many radar bearings the navigator would give the course and speed necessary to intercept the enemy, and we would roar off. It was fun, this game of cat-and-mouse, but I was still on the floor of the bridge and very curious to know what was happening. After each run Smithie would call to Number One and myself to come up and have a look. We were often amazed by the accuracy of an interception, but then there were other times when our enemy was in the opposite direction. Returning at 1600, we felt very radar-minded and keen to discover other wonders of the set.

Landing Smithie, we next took on Lieutenant Stratton Long, RNVR, the Gunnery Officer, and with much booming and banging we departed in true gunnery fashion. People were yelling at me from all directions. From the forward gun came: "Pom-pom loaded, latch set to safe;" from the opposite direction: "Oerlikon gun closed up, loaded, and latch set to safe." Two voices wafted in from port and starboard, "Vickers .303 guns loaded and set to safe." With full speed we roared toward the gun target, Number One and Long putting the gunnery crews through the paces. The teamwork between the gunners and the bridge developed noticeably. The first time we passed the target the signal for open fire was sounded. Nothing happened; we passed the target in silence. So the signal for cease fire was sounded. Then, much to the consternation of the Gunnery Officer and myself, there was a loud bang. Cease fire was again sounded, mingled with strong language from the bridge. We turned around and made another run for the target, hoping this time that there would be less confusion. The order was given to fire single shots only, and everything went off according to plan. Cease fire was given, and, miraculously, the guns stopped! The old target was surely laughing at us, as the shots fell every which way, but it didn't worry Long or the Gunnery Instructor. They were too busy explaining to the gunnery crews how to aim off as the ship rolled. *459* ran up and down past the target, and under Lieutenant Stratton Long's magic touch the gunners gained accuracy. MTB *459* was fast becoming an effective warship.

We sped back to harbour, fascinated by the water glistening as if covered with diamonds and the rocky coast bathed in a brilliant hue of orange by the setting sun. Anxious as we were to tuck into the rationed British meal and then relax, we knew that our work was not complete. There was yet another exercise —night interception by radar. An hour after the little trawler which was to be our target had departed, *459* edged her careful way out of the gloomy harbour, passing the navigation lights strung out into the Irish Sea. The object of this trip was to carry out a patrol along the "enemy" coast. We moved quietly down the imaginary convoy route, carrying out an all-round radar sweep. Smithie was on board again, and in the darkness we needed little to create the feeling that we were searching off a real enemy coast. The silencers were on and the engines purred contentedly. Half an hour passed. We picked up an echo. Excitedly we plotted course and speed, and the interception course was set. The boats were running in Order 4 (parallel to each other) for the torpedo attack. *459* illuminated the sky with starshells, silhouetting the little target. Two star cartridges were fired to represent the torpedo attack, and flashes from an Aldis lamp simulated gunfire. At the conclusion of the "violent battle", exhausted yet happy crews returned to the base. Thus ended our initial working-up day. Before long we began to recognize our qualities and limitations, and to realize that the road to becoming a fighting ship was a long and arduous one.

One bright March afternoon at about 1600, in blew Daddy Bones in *461* and Dave Killam in *460*, each executing a graceful circle before making fast alongside *459*. We were no longer alone, but had old comrades beside us; and being together we felt more like a flotilla. Day after day we drilled ourselves on station-keeping, a most vital factor in gun boat or torpedo boat warfare. The closer the boats kept together, in whatever formation was ordered, the better chance for a victorious engagement; and there was less danger of losing each other at night. So successful were our efforts in this direction that one day while running in Order 7 (all boats stationed on the starboard quarter of the Senior Officer's boat), I opened a packet of cigarettes, took one, and threw the packet over to Daddy Bones, who lit up and tossed the pack on to Dave Killam's boat. While we were doing this little trick our boats were travelling at 24 knots. During this exercise I recalled Lieutenant C.D.K. Richards, RN, the pioneer of close station-keeping, who achieved great success in the Strait of Dover before he met his death in battle against the heavily armed German flak trawlers.

The flotilla grew with the passing weeks. Bobby Moyse of *463*, Bishop (*464*), Charley Chaffey (*465*), and Glen Creba (*462*) had arrived. Barney Marshall (*466*) had still to put in an appearance, and we were beginning to be afraid he would never get around to the working-up base. We pictured him as being too busy bribing the Admiralty to install a six-pounder gun, or bigger and better torpedoes. As the 29th began to take shape, the COs attended frequent

Fired torpedo being recovered, Holyhead. These practice torpedoes were fitted with "blowing heads" and came to the surface at the end of their run emitting a plume of smoke to make location easier. (PAC C127020)

lectures on tactics and the handling of their ships, the navigators were up to their ears in speed plotting and radar interceptions, and the gunnery crews were being put through a severe grilling. The radar operator dreamed of blips and scans all night, and the wireless telegraphists fell into their bunks haunted by the sounds of long breaks and obliques.

Then came a day when great excitement pervaded the base. A signal had been received from London to the effect that Vice-Admiral (later Admiral) P.W. Nelles, Chief of the Naval Staff, would soon visit the two Canadian Motor Torpedo Boat Flotillas. A conference was called by the Captain of the base, attended by the Training Officer and his staff, Kirkie, and myself. We arranged an elaborate programme at sea—weather permitting—as well as a big "do" in the training base itself. When the greatly anticipated morning arrived, the wind was blowing in gale-force proportions and white-caps crashed against the rocky shores. The men of the 65th and 29th Flotillas lined up on the jetty. We were all in our Number One uniforms, and looking our best. One thing worried Kirkie and me: the uniforms of the men, besides being all shades of blue, in many cases had non-regulation zippers in the sides. A Canadian officer finally informed us that this had been approved, though not officially, and our fears were laid to rest. After a long wait the Admiral's car hove in sight with the pennant on the radiator cap fluttering in the wind, and within a few minutes the Chief of Naval Staff and his aides were on the scene. The guard of honour presented arms, and after inspecting them the Admiral was introduced to the Commanding Officers of the flotillas. Following this we all fell in opposite our respective ship's companies and the Admiral carried out a tour of inspection, during which he spoke to many of the men. After the inspection Kirkie and I proceeded to the Captain's home, where a luncheon party had been arranged in the Admiral's honour. Conversation hummed across the table, and Admiral Nelles was attacked with a barrage of questions: when would we invade the continent? would our flotillas be operational by then? and so on. He gave us encouraging answers, but wisely did not commit himself. After lunch the party went back down to the docks, where the Admiral inspected *464*, Lieutenant Bishop's boat. He seemed to be enjoying himself as he climbed up and down the narrow hatches, and he displayed a keen interest in the men and their work. He chatted with the Motor Mechanic in the engine-room, and joked with the Chief before leaving to carry out a tour of the bridge, chart-house, and radar cabin. He stopped to ask about each new gadget, often contributing an amusing comment. A clean-cut young lad standing rigidly to attention in the wireless cabin was soon put at ease by a question about his home town. Nelles spoke to all the crews during his tour. After he had signed the ship's log, *464* piped him over the side and saluted smartly. As he left the boat, Admiral Nelles said, "Best of luck and good actions to you all. I wish I were going with you."

Next on the programme was *748*, Kirkpatrick's boat, and here again a thorough inspection was carried out. The weather was still violent so the sea programme was off, but to give the Admiral an idea of the sea-going qualities of the boats, it was decided that he should put to sea in *748*, a 'D' class Fairmile, for a short trip outside the harbour. Following that the Admiral transferred to *459*, and we helped him into a waterproof zoot-suit. As we sped into the outer harbour we found ourselves in very rough waters. Admiral Nelles's face became covered with salty spray, but his eyes were twinkling as he turned to me and said, "Go faster, faster." I pushed up the throttles as far as they would go, and *459* lifted high in the air. It was great fun at this speed (the whereabouts of your stomach was another thing), and we opened fire at the moored target in order to give the CNS some idea of our rapid firepower. In the meantime the Chief Motor Mechanic, Dawson, was tugging at my trouser leg to tell me that the boost was rather high and the revs were the same, so I swung around and headed for harbour, reducing speed as we neared the outer breakwater. The crews secured guns and lined ship, and with her pennant numbers flying from the yardarm and the brass sparkling in the sunlight, *459* made fast alongside Kirk's ship. Kirkie very kindly invited me along with the Admiral and his staff to board *748* for tea, and we had a pleasant time. Admiral Nelles had genuinely enjoyed his two trips and was extremely pleased with both flotillas. He expressed the hope that he would be able to visit us again, and said in his parting message, "I hope you soon meet the enemy with much success." As we watched the Admiral's car disappear through the gates, Kirkie and I felt confident in the future of the two Canadian flotillas.

The first battle had already begun for the 29th Flotilla, and it was a losing battle . . . against the Admiralty. Prior to the visit of the CNS a signal had arrived which stated that the 29th's torpedo tubes were to be removed and depth-charge racks fitted. Our boats were to carry 48 small depth charges loaded with minol. It had all started when somebody in the Admiralty had gone into a panic over the German "W-Boat". This remarkable submarine, so called because it was powered with a Walter hydrogen peroxide fuelled turbine, was supposed to do 40 knots on the surface, and a still more fantastic 30 knots under water. According to the Admiralty, it had been designed as a precaution against invasion. Mere words cannot express the effect on the flotilla's morale—the bottom had dropped out of everything, and our faces were long and sad as we watched our main armament and striking power being taken away. How we were expected to deal with this mythical new boat now was not explained. All we had was a hydrophone, hanging primitively over the starboard side, which gave us only a very rough idea of where the noise was coming from. We were most anxious to know more about the mysterious W-Boat, but although we sought information on its design and use, no one could tell us a thing about the phantom craft. The matter was taken up with Admiral Nelles during his visit, and he and his staff promised to do all that they could when they returned to London.

In the meantime, there sat our little boats—unarmed—a hard blow! But there was no sense in moping, so we buckled down to devising plans for battling the strange new serpent of the narrow seas. For the remainder of the training period we practised high-speed anti-E- and R-Boat gunnery tactics. At this very time, the great invasion, which promised to be the mightiest military feat in all history, was about to begin. How, when, and where were alike unknown; but throughout the country obvious preparations were visible, and for us the tense period of waiting had set in. Indeed, the whole world was waiting . . . and here was the 29th, weaponless, and up to its neck in fairy tales about W-Boats.

Every cloud does have its silver lining. One day the Training Commander called me up to his office to give me some good news. Not only did he consider MTBs *459, 460,* and *461* to be fully worked up, but he also informed me that *460,* Dave Killam's boat, had won the award given to the most efficient gunnery crew. This was the first time for several months that a boat in the Allied MTBs had met the required and extremely high standards—few boats in Coastal Force had ever won this efficiency prize. This was the first feather in the 29th's cap, and we were all highly pleased, particularly the crew of Dave's boat. The Training Commander had been very impressed with the manner in which the

Opposite: MTB 459 during the working-up period at Holyhead. (PAC PA107900)

Canadians had entered into the spirit of the games organized to improve skill and fighting ability. Dave himself was a keen and effective officer and had set an excellent example of good team work for his men.

The time had come for the three boats to be separated, though only temporarily. Dave's boat was to refit at Holyhead before becoming operational, Daddy Bones's at Shoreham near Hove, and I was to go to British Power Boats at Poole, Dorset. We were to be based under the Dover Command at Ramsgate, and the remainder of the flotilla was to complete a few more weeks of working-up before joining us. A paymaster named Pinhorn (a most confusing name; more often than not it came out Pinpoint or Needlehead) announced in his high-pitched voice that he would proceed to Ramsgate to crack the ice before the boats arrived.

At 0700 Daddy Bones and I set sail in the chilly blackness. Guided by the flashing buoys, our small vessels felt their way out of the harbour, passed the breakwater for the last time, and sailed onto the convoy route, where we tangled with the odd merchant ship. We retraced our way down to Milford Haven, refuelled, and soon were sailing past the familiar Isle of Lundy. Daylight had since returned, and we gloried in the warm rays of the April sun. Rounding Land's End we encountered a large ocean swell coming in from the Atlantic, and it was thrilling to ride the heavy swells at 30 knots: *459* and *461* would momentarily lose nearly all sight of each other, with only the mast-heads visible, then the next moment *461* would tower above us, surfing down the swell. See-sawing in this way we headed for the little port of Penzance, and I noticed Daddy Bones's face and bald head gleaming with a glorious sunburn. Our crews carried out rifle practice as the boats bubbled along, but once all the cardboard boxes and bottles had been expended this exercise came to an end. Soon we were opposite Penzance and flashing madly to the shore base for the pilot boat. After many messages it finally appeared to lead us into the difficult harbour.

Next day a strong wind blew; it blew so hard we were blown into our favourite pub, the Station Hotel. Our stock with the proprietor there was extremely high, and he wined and dined us like kings. The following day we were able to sail, so we gently felt our way out of Penzance Channel. Once the craft were in open waters I whirled my arm over my head, signalling Daddy Bones for increased speed. With the revolutions pushed up the boats were soon planing over the smooth seas *en route* to Dartmouth. On our way we passed hundreds of landing craft of all shapes and sizes, chock-a-block with American troops, as well as many cruisers and destroyers, all heading for the sandy beach at the southern end of the Dartmouth coast to carry out a mock invasion exercise. Avoiding this armada, which covered the horizon, would have entailed circling eight or ten miles off our course, so I decided that we should weave our way through the bevy of strange and cumbersome vessels. A cruiser flashed us

MTB 459 during the working-up period at Holyhead. (PAC PA144587)

to ask what part we were playing in the mock invasion. Jokingly we replied that we were the E-Boats, and we got the signal to carry on. This was the first time I really felt the invasion to be close at hand.

Arriving at Dartmouth we called up the harbour and received permission to enter, and so wound our perilous way through the conglomeration of landing craft to make fast alongside the Coastal Force depot ship. We received our sailing orders shortly and left Dartmouth again, this time accompanied by a friend, Lieutenant Salmon, RNVR, the Commanding Officer of a gun boat. Known to the Coastal Force types as "Fish", he sported a fair beard and a pair of twinkling blue eyes. True to those eyes, he was always up to some mischief, and when he hadn't a natter on he had a drip about something.

Our three boats passed the gate at the harbour entrance and rounded the reef which was close to the mouth of the channel running toward Dartmouth. I was in the lead with Daddy Bones astern, and Fish was tail-end-Charlie. It was another fine day. The water mirrored the beautiful, rhythmic lines of the little boats as they planed along, bows thrust out of the sea, sending up a sparkling plume astern which foamed into an angry wake and broke the serenity of the waters. As we passed around Portland Bill, the chalk cliffs of Weymouth Bay came into view, and to the north we saw twelve large ships in line ahead, their white funnels reflected in the sun. Sailing by these ships, we recognized them as large landing-craft carriers of the type that would bear shock troops into an invasion. They, too, were carrying out invasion practices. Aircraft roared busily overhead, laying a thick white smokescreen between us and Poole, our destination. Daddy Bones, deciding that he would ply on to the Needles, making for the Solent and thence to Shoreham, bade us farewell, and *459* replied with, "A successful refit and good leave." Daddy Bones sped on, and soon became a tiny silhouette with a mighty wake. In the meantime, the aircraft, not satisfied with one layer of smoke, proceeded to make a dozen more. I switched on my radar and told Fish to do the same, for our two boats were soon in the thick of the smoke, which stung our faces and made us all weep like babies.

Before long it was impossible to see as far as the stern, and after an uncomfortable and nerve-racking four miles of enveloping white smoke, *459* found herself face to face with the white cliffs of Anvil Point. Rubbing the tears out of our eyes we sighted Fish looming up out of the smoke some miles away, so we sped onward past the chalk-white minarets, slowing down to flash Fish to take the lead up the tricky channel to Poole. The Naval Officer in Charge flashed us from shore, and after observing the formalities he signalled us to wait for the pilot he would send. Half an hour passed, and there was still no pilot boat. Fish was becoming very impatient, and his beard was waggling fast as a flow of uncensored words took to the air. He brought his boat alongside mine and shouted, "The damn pilot will never be here. He only had four miles to come. I know this channel like a book, so follow me." Accordingly, with "Pilot" Salmon in the lead, the two boats sailed slowly up the meandering channel and through the congested harbour of Poole.

I was summoned to the office of the Naval Officer in Charge forthwith, and arriving in good time was ushered in to find myself face to face with a delightful boffin who must have served in the Boer War. To his blast for coming up the harbour without a pilot, I replied timidly that I had had an excellent substitute pilot, who had taken many ships up and down those tricky waters. The dear old Commander explained, "Matter of fact, old boy, it makes the pilot rather annoyed to go all the way down there for nothing; he's a civilian and has to pay for his own petrol." I replied that in that case, as Lieutenant

MTB 459 during the working-up period at Holyhead. (PAC PA128275)

Salmon knew the pilot well, the two of us would square off the matter. This we did in the Antelope Inn, so named for the stuffed animal at the entrance. It was a marvellous pub, full of character. There was a parrot in one corner of the barroom, and a spherical soul behind the bar. The owner of the pub was a short, stocky fellow, who had the habit when speaking of peering over the glasses which were perilously perched on the end of his nose. Fish, as usual, was full of mischief, and the pilot and myself were soon feeling no pain. By the time the evening was over, diplomatic relations were so good that we even signed the pilot's log book.

CHAPTER THREE

INITIATION BY FIRE

MTB *459'S* REFIT WAS OVER, and under the supervision of scores of Admiralty geniuses she had completed her depth-charge trials. They had shaken the poor old boat's innards so vigorously that all the electric light bulbs and the wireless and radar tubes were smashed, and she had staggered in suffering from the shock, but still bearing up nobly. After two unpleasant weeks she was free to make her way down the narrow channel of Poole, and she looked very special indeed. Her sides had been painted a glorious robin's-egg blue and her decks contrasted handsomely in darker blue. On each side were the new depth-charge rails, which slightly marred her streamlined appearance, and she was burdened with 48 annoying depth charges.

We had just rounded the narrow point on our last lap when I noticed the whizzing of shells overhead and saw them crashing in the sand dunes to starboard. Some were falling short, and to me they seemed uncomfortably close. Two destroyers were sitting in Bournemouth Bay delighting themselves by putting shells over our heads. Doubtful of their gunnery, we flashed, "Request you cease fire."

"Can't take it, eh?" came back the answer.

"Pick on someone your own size," I retorted.

With that the firing ceased, and we steamed on out of range, passing the last buoy in the tricky Poole channel and planing on through the Solent toward Dover at an easy 30 knots.

We had a distinguished passenger with us on this trip, Lieutenant Tom Wood, RCNVR, one of the Official Canadian Naval War Artists, and he seemed to be enjoying the jaunt immensely. Throughout the Solent we were amazed by the number of ships at anchor—battleships, cruisers, destroyers, merchant ships, and landing craft by the hundreds. Hospital ships, their glaring white splotched with huge red crosses, acknowledged our tiny craft as she passed by. The sight of this great armada sent shivers down my spine. How soon would the signal be sent to set this fleet in motion? Other strange objects were being pushed and pulled by tugs just off the beaches of the Solent. Some of these appeared to be bridges, others were just giant cement blocks with anti-aircraft guns mounted on top. Floating cement made no sense at all, yet there they were, with five tugs each nursing them into place.

Although the sun was trying desperately to shine through, it was still foggy as we passed East Solent Gate on the way to Ramsgate, near Dover. *459* had to depend on her radar as she buoy-hopped up the coast to South Foreland. From there on, the blanket of fog behind us, we sailed in brilliant sunlight through the dangerous Goodwin Sands to Ramsgate. In the quaint harbour we made fast alongside the rest of the flotilla, which had been arriving boat by boat over the past few weeks. All were present except Bones.

Opposite: Liberty men ashore. (PAC C127044)

I had no sooner set foot ashore than I learned of a big hush-hush operation which was on the programme for that night. All the officers were tense, and I knew the operation must be important, but it was out of the question to take *459* as she still had defects and her QH Navigational Aid set was not wired. Bobby Moyse was very keen about the whole thing, and I hinted that I should be going in his boat as a passenger to gain experience. He quickly invited me on board, and in the meantime I had all my gear sent up to the Mess and located the large room which contained the sleeping quarters. The other occupants were Polish officers, and what with their rather shaky English and my non-existent Polish, conversation was necessarily limited. After a hasty clean-up and dinner, I joined Bobby to get further details on the night's operation.

Bobby, Dave Killam, Bishop, Barney Marshall, Chuff-Chuff (Charlie Chaffey), and little Glen Creba were all down for the "do". At 1800 the 29th Flotilla slipped out of the harbour in line-ahead formation *en route* to Dover for further secret briefings. The sky was filled with clouds soaking in the golden rays of the sinking sun, the waters were tinted with flame, and the chalk cliffs had turned cool cobalt blue with hints of rose. In the midst of all this splendour the crews were tense, for it was the first operation of this nature they had taken part in. Bobby led the boats slowly through to the inner harbour of Dover and into the submarine basin. On the right was a huge reinforced-concrete structure with a cement roof 14 feet thick. Fourteen pens beneath the roof provided shelter for the MTBs, and from each pen ran a ladder leading to the sleeping quarters. The boats made fast to the east side of the wall, above which towered the famous chalk cliffs and the Dover Castle. In the bowels of the cliff far beneath this ancient castle lay the nerve centre of Dover Command.

Bobby and I climbed to the top of the jetty and walked to the bomb-proof pens, where in the wardroom I was besieged by many of my Coastal Force comrades: Lieutenant Arnold Foster, DSO, DSC, RNVR, Senior Officer of a flotilla of MTBs; old Fergy, an Australian; Pluggie, another Senior Officer; and some of the Dutch officers. The other members of the Mess were Army, some identifiable as Canadians by their flashes, already dressed in the Army's version of sea-going togs and ready to go. Many of the lads had blackened their faces for this strange operation.

All the characters gathered in the Operations Room. The atmosphere was both exciting and alarming. The Chief of Staff and the Senior Officer of Operations briefly outlined the plans. I had noticed when entering the pens that some of the MTBs were fitted with little dinghies equipped with small engines, and we now learned that these boats would be escorted by the 29th Canadian Flotilla, given the job because of its firepower and QH sets, the latest thing in navigation. This instrument could put us within 25 yards of absolute accuracy in our position. The boats were divided into four groups. One of these was assigned to a position a few miles south of Boulogne, another would go under the Calais guns at Cap Blanc, a third was to proceed north of Calais harbour, and the remaining group was to be sent to a point near Dunkirk. Army engineering officers were to be landed on each of several beaches with the object of securing and returning with one of the enemy's mines; it was extremely important that samples of the various types of mines planted on the beaches by the enemy be obtained and studied so that some method of disabling them could be found, thus simplifying to some degree the first steps of the planned gigantic invasion. All navigators' watches were synchronized and the final details were arranged. We walked slowly out of the Operations Room, buttoning up sea-gear as we went, and then moved toward our respective boats, looking like shadowy phantoms in the dark. Engine after engine roared to life, shattering the stillness of the cool night air, and shouts of "Cast off!" added to the din. Black silhouettes filed out of the harbour and separated, each on his own mission.

The wind started to blow and the weather became increasingly nasty. Bobby and I were on the bridge, our eyes straining into the murky darkness watching for navigation buoys. The British MTBs carrying the army officers

(PAC PA144580)

were crashing along on our starboard side. At times we could scarcely see them. The spray flew thick and heavy as we plied on past Ramsgate and altered course to seaward. Dumbton buoy loomed into sight, and we set course for Dunkirk. Heavy waves smashed against the tiny vessel. The water slapped our faces with stinging blows, then trickled irritatingly down our necks to fill our boots; and with the crash of each mighty wave we felt our spines vibrate cruelly. The little group on the bridge of *462* was truly a miserable lot. Finally it was decided that under current weather conditions it would be impossible to carry out the tricky operation, and a signal was sent to Supreme Command at Dover. Similar complaints poured in from the other units; one could hear the chattering Morse code in the wireless cabinet pouring out messages of woe. It wasn't long before Supreme Command replied, "Return to harbour," and gratefully we turned 180° to retrace our course through the darkness back to Dover. We spent the night there, ready to begin the operation again on 15 minutes' notice. The sun rose at last, and dirty and unshaven, with sleep still clinging to our clothes, we stepped into our boats to glide home over the now glassy water to Ramsgate. As soon as the little ships were docked, the crews headed for their quarters to bathe, change, and breakfast, and the officers were not far behind.

It was a beautiful May morning. Ramsgate had not yet awakened, and the base was eking out its last few minutes of slumber before beginning the humdrum work of the day. Overhead, the barrage balloons, relaxed and motionless, had yet to come to life. We officers, stubble-faced and weary-eyed, trudged up the hill to the Mess, our footsteps echoing in the stillness of the early dawn. On top of the hill the Mess, which had once been the Royal Ramsgate Yacht Club, stood out in all its dignity. Its interior was filled with yellowed pictures of bygone yachting days. Here, too, sleep still reigned supreme, and our footsteps sounded abnormally loud in the silent corridors. But the quiet was soon broken by Bobby Moyse as he satirically recalled the amusing incidents of the night's operation and we all burst into fits of laughter. Dave Killam gave forth with his story of the night's activity south of Boulogne, and with all the chit-chat back and forth the Yacht Club gradually acknowledged the new day. Soon the flow of water into the bathtubs and the splashing sounds in basins blended cheerily with the chatter.

I found myself refreshed after a good breakfast, and soon settled down to solving my flotilla's main problems. First on the list was the job of redecorating the hotel which had been allocated as crew space. It was a new building, and smart in appearance, but the interior was badly in need of a coat of calcium since our predecessors had left it in a terribly unclean state. Before long I had a working party busy scrubbing out the place from top to bottom, and as soon as each room had been cleaned, a second working party, armed with large brushes,

(PAC PA 136833)

took over and transformed it to a lovely buff colour. Next came the question of food. Canadians were not accustomed to the small rations which sufficed the British ratings, and diplomacy was required in approaching the Royal Navy Victualling Officer. The problem was satisfactorily solved when the Victualling Officer agreed to issue more hot meals in the evenings before the crews went to sea. There was much correspondence to be attended to as well, including one important letter which was aimed at getting our own Canadian rations. When this task had been completed, planning of the night's operation followed. The Senior Officer Operations rang me from Dover to say that the same boats would make a second attempt at last night's mission since they were already briefed and knew the score. There was a repeat briefing at 1700 to ensure that the most up-to-date enemy information was known. This time I decided not to go to sea as a spectator, but instead to try to catch up on matters concerning the flotilla.

Bobby Moyse, Dave Killam, Bishop, and Chuff-Chuff sailed at sundown for Dover, where they joined their Army comrades and escorted them across the Channel. The operation was successful. The Army landed at different points off the French coast and managed to procure an enemy mine from each of the beaches. Having returned to its MTB, the small boat in each case was hoisted aboard and the mine was gently secured. At Dover the mines were loaded aboard a truck, and the Army, with its new German toys, drove off in triumph to London.

By the middle of May the flotilla had settled down. The crew's hotel, known as HMCS *Canada,* was humming with life. Bunks had been installed, augmented with odd bits of scrounged furniture, and pin-up girls glamorized the clean buff walls. The boats had been fitted with the most modern equipment, and the flotilla was itching for its first taste of action. My commanding officers and I spent our mornings in the Tactical Asdic truck devising ways and means to defeat the mysterious W-Boat, which by this time had thoroughly aroused everyone's curiosity. It still had not been established as a fact.

One night at about this time, the Naval Mess had reached what seemed the peak of activity. As the 29th Canadian MTB Flotilla was not required for sea, the two-by-four bar resounded with jovial voices, laughter, and other related sounds of gaiety. Above the fireplace hung a German naval ensign, appropriately drilled with holes, beneath which was an oil painting by Ronnie Barge of Lieutenant Richards's flotilla. To the right of this picture hung another large oil painting, depicting Ramsgate harbour filled with yachts and paddlewheel steamers. Gay characters dolled up in the colourful styles of the nineties strolled on the shore.

Bobby Moyse was in excellent form, telling one of his Russian stories complete with accent and gestures. Bish was neatly dressed, as usual, with a white handkerchief in his breast pocket and his hair slicked down, and was madly attempting to order the one and only taxi in Ramsgate. It was the flotilla's night off and we were all invited to a birthday party for a Wren named Pat, which was to be held at the Wheat Sheaf Inn near Margate. The fellows were all in the mood for a party: Chuff-Chuff, no longer his usual quiet self, wore a cherubic smile, and continually chirped entertaining comments in a low voice; and Barney Marshall was raring to go. We were no longer on our dignity, and the English officers were highly amused by our antics and the Canadian lingo. Before many minutes had passed, a sedate and elderly gentleman, clad in a grey Scotch tweed suit, unobtrusively walked in to politely enquire, "Pardon me, Sir, which gentleman ordered a taxi?"

With screams of "We all did!" there was a mad scramble out of the bar, down the steps, and into the taxi. The vehicle closely resembled a royal limousine of about 1921 vintage. Once we were all aboard the driver set out cautiously through the darkened streets of Ramsgate. When we reached the highway the car sped up to its maximum of 15 miles an hour, although when it came to an incline it would shift to low gear and creep up. The voices inside, raised in song, kept time with the racing engine, and clouds of oil fumes spouted forth on every hill. Eventually, the taxi drew up with dignity in front of the inn, and we fell out in all directions. The dear old driver asked us what time he should return, and thanking him profusely, I replied, "10:30 please."

Ironized MacGoffoneys (see page 52) went along to the party at the Wheat Sheaf Inn. (PAC PA127047)

Pat and her party had arrived before us and the celebration was well under way. It was my first visit to the Wheat Sheaf Inn, and I was pleasantly surprised by the cheerful, homey atmosphere. In the centre of the room was a large table surmounted by an ornate floral arrangement, oriental rugs covered the floor, and big, comfortable easy chairs were scattered about. The oak-panelled walls were covered with Henry VIII prints and brass "tally-ho" bugles. On one side was a plate rack, filled with fine examples of Crown Derby. Pat was a pretty little thing with fair hair and a golden suntan, and she looked very smart in her Wren uniform. Mind you, there were other Pats—the girls all seemed to have that name—but she was *the* Pat. Voices were soon raised in song with "Cardinal Puff-Puff" and "Chug-a-Lug", priming the party for a good sing-song, and by this time everyone in the pub, including the barmaids, had joined in. The singing was something out of this world. Bobby was at the peak of his story-telling and a young English lad was doing a fine job of reciting "Eskimo Nell" when we heard the restrained voice of our taxi driver through the gaiety and laughter. Regretfully, we bade adieu to the barmaids, the Army, the Air Force, and to all who had joined in the friendly little party. The manager of the pub and the barmaids thanked us for coming with our songs and laughter and hoped that we would come again. Having staggered into the limousine, we were off in a cloud of smoke.

May was passing by quickly. The invasion was the mainstay of all conversation, and more strange edifices were being built in the area. Daddy Bones had still not joined us. He was involved in a slaphappy refit at Shoreham, near Brighton, and the delay had become so exasperating that poor Bones was nearly driven around the bend. Bobby, whose boat *462* had been damaged in the bow, had sailed for Poole, and he was frantic for fear of missing the great day. I managed to get him off to British Power Boats for repairs, which they estimated would take five days to complete. In the meantime, Dave Killam, Bish, Chuff-Chuff, Glen Creba, and I were holding the fort with nightly patrols. As the days had gone by the flotilla had become more operation-minded, but as yet there had been no conflicts with the enemy. We were envious of the Dutch gun boats commanded by Little Willie Delouise. They had achieved a good record at Dover, working very hard and going to sea every night without slackening their pace. We often watched the small, odd-looking Motor Anti-Submarine Boats which laid the smokescreen for every daylight convoy going through the Strait of Dover, to protect the ships from the enemy's heavy guns at Calais and Cap Gris Nez.

The 22nd of May 1944 dawned hot and hazy, with air so softly hued that even the edges of the chalk cliffs seemed indefinite. The sun poured down on the MTBs in the quiet waters of the harbour. The Senior Officer Operations at Dover called me up, "Is that you, Law?"

"Yes, Sir."

"Good," he continued, "I want four of your boats tonight for an operation off the enemy coast. Also two boats for patrol. Can you give me their numbers?"

"MTBs *459,* the Senior Officer's boat, *464, 465,* and *466.* And for the patrol, *460,* Lieutenant Killam as Senior Officer, and *462.*"

"Good. Briefing at 1700 this afternoon for the four boats for operation off the French coast." I thanked him, and after hanging up banged out a signal informing the boats concerned that they would be required for sea duty and a briefing at 1700. The day was spent preparing equipment and checking the ships to be sure they were ready for sea. John Shand, with Joe Adams, Vern Barlow, and Joe Bampton, was busy marking all the latest minefields and dispositions of buoys on their charts, as well as gathering all possible information concerning the tides on the enemy coast. The wireless operators checked to see that call signs were up to date, and the gunners loaded starshell ammunition for the pom-pom gun. Everyone was sweating in the hot summer sun to ensure that the boats were operational. Spirits ran high, and the air was tense with the feeling that we were about to have our first taste of action. The crews and officers had an early supper, and at 1615 the officers sauntered slowly down from the Yacht Club around the western arm to where the boats lay. The engines, roaring as they warmed up, sounded like a fleet of dive bombers attacking the town, and the white cliffs shook with the vibration. *459, 464, 465,* and *466* were to proceed at 1630 to Dover, where the briefing would be held beneath the ancient castle.

Wearing my Gieves flotation suit plus many extra clothes, I could hardly breathe. The chill Channel air forced us to dress warmly, and I always found it cold at sea, even in summer. Climbing down the ladder, I found the crew ready to slip moorings. Dressed in their black zoot-suits and RCN life-jackets, their

shapes were so distorted they looked like a flock of "ironized MacGoffoneys", those mysterious beings who were blamed whenever one of the MTBs had an otherwise inexplicable mechanical problem. My boat, *459*, hoisted the "Preparative to Slip", and when all the answering pennants were hoisted, Lovelock, my signalman, hauled the message down again with a quick and professional touch as if we were a battleship.

The boats moved slowly out of harbour and took up their stations. The ship's company dressed ship with the First Lieutenant standing in the bow. Crews fell out and closed up to action stations on the double, as they had practised many times in drill. Gunners shouted, "Guns loaded, latch to safe." We increased speed over the unbroken waters, past the familiar target (a sunken ship's mast), and performed our routine practice gun-shoot. There was a loud booming and clattering, the area became thick with tracer and falling shell, and the flotilla was rather pleased with all the hits achieved. Then we were on our way again through the mist, and before long the entrance to Dover loomed up through the muggy air. The boats made fast near the MTB pens, and I stripped off my sea-going clothes down to my oldest uniform—the one with the green buttons—and an old, salty cap which was my pet. Bish, Chuff-Chuff, Barney Marshall, Lieutenant Plugge (Senior Officer of the accompanying flotilla), and I climbed the ladder to the waiting car, and drove through the dockyard and down the narrow streets of Dover. Ruined buildings flanked our route—monuments to Dover's sacrifice. We wound up the steep hill to the castle, crossed the moat, and passed through the ancient gates where the car was stopped for the usual identity card routine. Our voices and footsteps were soon echoing sharply in the long tunnels as we made our way toward the Operations Room, where the

Manoeuvres off Dover. (PAC C127040)

Chief of Staff and the Senior Officer Operations were waiting. The Chief of Staff opened the conversation by informing us that he expected a small convoy escorted by four enemy "LCT Mk 4s". These had originally been designed by the Germans as landing craft, but as times and conditions changed, they were employed as flak ships, armed with 88-mm, 20-mm, and 37-mm guns, which were equally effective against air and surface targets, and thus created stiff opposition for Coastal Force. The convoy, which would probably include flak trawlers and E- or R-Boats, was expected at 2330 off Berk Buoy. Plugge was to set his torpedoes at minimum depth. After the Chief of Staff had discussed the courses and time of departure, he introduced me to Admiral Commanding Dover, Admiral Pridham-Wippell. The Admiral quickly put me at ease, and I departed after a short conversation. Back on board I was greeted with the usual hundred-octane gasoline fumes as the engines bellowed forth. The western sun had slipped gently behind the chalk cliffs. Bish, Chuff-Chuff, and Marshall were on their bridges, donning their warm clothes and checking that binoculars and signal lamps were close at hand. The testing of wireless communication could be heard over the vibration of the engines. Signal was given to slip.

Lieutenant Plugge's boat, *354,* came out of the pen stern-first, followed by *361, 362,* and *358.* One had the impression that the pens were large apartment houses where people lived above and kept their cars below, and that all the MTBs were backing out of their garages. The 3rd British MTB Flotilla, Plugge's, slipped into line-ahead formation. For this operation they went under the name of "Group Able". The 29th was "Group Baker". The little fleet passed the entrance and the 29th formed up on its starboard side. I was abreast of the Senior Officer. Because I was a newcomer to Dover and on my first operation, Lieutenant Plugge was the Senior Officer while I was just Senior Officer for the 29th Canadian MTBs. The boats were in two columns of line-ahead, approximately 200 yards apart, a most difficult formation with the low visibility. The speed was set at 25 knots. There was no horizon and the night was black and mysterious. We moved past Folkestone to the outer Lade Buoy, altered course to East Bullock Buoy situated in the middle of the Channel opposite Dungeness, and then re-altered course down toward Berk. Visibility was rapidly deteriorating and our station-keeping became more difficult. At 2330 we reached Berk Buoy, about five miles off the French coast, where we again altered course and ran south, parallel to the enemy coast. Travelling the German convoy route at a speed of eight knots, the patrol ran to and fro on a ten-mile stretch south of the Berk Buoy. This placed us in a strategic position for our radar sweeps.

I felt in my bones that tonight we should meet the enemy. Cold chills chased one another unpleasantly up and down my spine. Even Leading Seaman French, my coxswain, sensed the impending fireworks. I told him he should be careful with the large red pom-pom decorating his white toque; it might be shot off. He answered with a smile, "If it comes that close I won't have to worry." The radar rating carried out a continuous, careful sweep as the column of ships moved down to the southern end of the patrol, where we altered course to steam north retracing our way toward the buoy. At this point, as we altered course 180°, three of Plugge's boats—*358, 361,* and *362*—lost us. The poor visibility conditions had made it impossible for them to stay in the exceedingly difficult formation. The remaining boats reached the northern end of the patrol with no success in finding the enemy. Dover was usually surprisingly accurate with convoy times, but tonight the convoy was late. The five of us waited; we were in a vulnerable position should we meet the enemy. With the low visibility, I was afraid that if an action started we would be unable to tell friend from foe. To top things off, Senior Officer Group Able developed engine trouble, and was forced to go seaward to clear the area. At the same time, a starshell blossomed to the south, dead ahead. Another appeared . . . it was the familiar German starshell, greenish in colour and brilliant with candlepower. Group Baker rushed immediately to action stations.

I called down the voice pipe to Simpson, the radar operator, "Can you see anything on your set? Two starshells are bearing dead ahead."

"Scan clear, Sir."

I told him to continue his sweep and to watch ahead carefully.

By this time my heart was pounding loudly and fast. I called up Bish, Chuff-Chuff, and Barney and told them to go into battle formation, Order 7, which means taking up station on the Senior Officer's port quarter. Our little group of four slowly moved down toward the south, while all eyes peered through binoculars, straining to pick out dark shapes against a hazy horizon.

I was worried; the three MTBs at large to the south posed a handicap as they might be in our way and certainly were not in a position to aid us. More starshells suddenly lit up the night sky ahead and slightly to the port bow. An enthusiastic call burst up from the radar king: "Echo bearing Green 10 [10° to starboard], 3000 yards, amplitude three times."

"How many?" I asked.

"Four, and several small indistinct echoes."

As we closed on the enemy, starshells filled the sky, illuminating the area as if it were some giant amphitheatre. Tracers came from dead ahead, and in the light of the starshells we identified three objects at Green 10 as the three British MTBs disengaging from the enemy. This was a great relief, for Group Baker was now free to act. Our four boats increased speed to 25 knots and bore down on the enemy. Radar bearings and ranges poured faster and faster up to the bridge as we closed. Through my binoculars I could see four low flak barges. The MTBs roared through the water, while overhead the sky brightened as our red starshells mingled with the enemy's green ones, scattering their colourful, dangerous tracers. The battle was on!

The pom-poms were blazing away as our tiny ships closed the ugly black phantoms. Heavy 88-mm anti-personnel shells burst above our heads, leaving angry puffs of black smoke. Others exploded nearby, sending up gigantic needle-shaped columns of water. Green and red tracers, brilliant and terrifying missiles of death, flew through the air in graceful arcs toward our vulnerable wooden vessels. They danced over the waters, hitting with sharp, resounding crackles. By this time the noise had reached its climax and the smell of cordite was overpowering. A shell falling close near the bow of *464* left small splinters in her bow, shot away Bish's ensign, and damaged the bridge and flag lockers. Marshall was attacked by small, high-speed craft, which were apparently being used for the first time; certainly I'd never come across them before. Having closed the enemy to 300 yards we went into Order 1 (line-ahead) and brought all our guns to bear broadside on the foe. The battle was hot and fierce. Our tiny craft were fighting gamely against a superior and furious enemy, and the good Lord alone knows why we were not all sunk.

(PAC PA144574)

Coxswain French and I ducked in unison each time a red tracer shell came too close, and our heads often banged together in the confusion. Old Shand was yelling for course at the top of his lungs. The radar rating shouted out bearings. The wireless operator called the bridge to ask if the last message should be sent in code. But all in vain were their pleas, for no individual voice could be distinguished in the roar of the battle.

Group Baker turned about and disengaged to catch its breath and lick its wounds. As the sounds of the battle diminished I could hear John Shand. Turning to French at the wheel, I said, "For God's sake, give him a course quickly so he'll pipe down!"

The coxswain replied, "Course West, Sir."

Old John wanted to know what had caused the awful rumpus and confusion. Regaining our composure, we sent the formal signals to Dover stating that we had been in action and reporting the damage we thought had been done to our rather rough opponents. I called up the boys to find out if there were any casualties, and Bish replied that his boat had been slightly damaged. He had gone into action with his ensign, but had come out without it. The 29th pulled up its socks and decided to give chase to the enemy. By this time I had managed to stop my knees from banging together and my breath was back, and all in all I felt much braver. To my amazement the coxswain's toque still sported its red pom-pom, and when I asked him why he had not worn his tin hat, he replied that there had not been enough time to put it on. Embarrassed, I suddenly realized I did not have mine on either. I found that it always fell over my eyes, causing a complete blackout and leaving me without the vaguest notion of what was happening.

We moved slowly to the northeast, hoping to pay our nasty friends another visit. They hadn't spared themselves with their reception. As the boats increased speed, our gunners reloaded, keen to give the Jerries more than before. The empty shells rolled from side to side with the ship's motion, playing a jangling, discordant symphony as they crashed about. Simpson, the radar operator, shouted that he had an echo. Group Baker was off again, tin helmets adjusted.

The echo was dead ahead, 2000 yards. We altered course, and the echo altered course. We increased speed; it increased speed. We reduced speed; and it did the same. Something odd was going on. A few starshells disclosed nothing. The echo then bore down upon us . . . and disappeared. The radar operator called up to the bridge, "Excuse me, Sir, but I think it's another one of those ironized MacGoffoneys." I was beginning to think the same. We sniffed around, looking for the elusive enemy, and soon found ourselves approaching the RAF bombing area. MTBs were forbidden to enter this zone, a line well south of Boulogne to Cap Gris Nez, so I decided that we should head for home and leave it to the Air Force to dice up the enemy.

Before arriving home we held a rendezvous to discuss over the loud hailer exactly what had happened in the engagement, so the 29th could give Senior Officer Operations a consistent account of the proceedings. One naughty officer had gone off on his own after one of the strange, small, high-speed craft, a proceeding which is strictly not according to the books, and during the action he had engaged the mysterious boat with light-calibre guns. This left the conference to Bish, Chuff-Chuff, and myself. Chuff-Chuff said that he had seen the strange craft, and, if I remember correctly, Bish wasn't sure. I myself hadn't seen the small skimmers because the four large LCT Mk 4s had taken up all my time and attention. In the thick of the action, it had been impossible to obtain a complete picture of the encounter, and the flash-pictures on the screen of my memory glimpsed only the highlights of the action. We all agreed that there had been many hits on the enemy. After all accounts had been given, Footsie and I tried to piece the whole engagement together. It was like working out a jigsaw puzzle, and the high-speed craft were hardest to fit into the picture. It had been rumoured that the enemy possessed such a vessel, but as yet there had been no reports of its having been used.

In high spirits, glad to be alive, the little MTBs pursued their homeward course. The sun rose in the east, tinting the sky and water and distant land a warm pink, and the morale of the flotilla rose with it. The nightmare had passed. We had had our initiation by fire. The action had not been a great success, but it had been creditable. The three boats, pennant numbers flying, came proudly alongside their familiar berth, and we noted that the bad boy of the flotilla was already home.

The engines of the four boats had scarcely shut down before the crews gathered into a single group, everyone talking at once and inspecting each other's boats to see who had sustained the most damage. The crew of the boat which had not been in on the operation came running down to get the news of the night's frolic. Some of the gunners were patting their guns with pride, their teeth sparkling in faces black with cordite. Amazed at their eagerness so early in the morning, I watched as they started to clean their guns, which were soon shimmering in the sunlight with a fresh coat of oil. Excitement was running so high that it was hard for the boys to settle down. I congratulated John Shand, my Number One, on his excellent navigation, using the traditional, "Good work," to which he replied with a slow grin, "Why, naturally!"

I had received a message that I was to ring the Senior Officer Operations as soon as I landed. Thinking he wouldn't be too pleased with the night's effort, I picked up the phone and in a far from self-assured voice asked to speak to the Senior Officer. He had been up all night in the castle, and his voice, as it came over the wire, contained the same tired hoarseness as if he had just been awakened from a deep sleep. Much to my amazement he seemed delighted as I

(PAC PA144590)

gave him a brief outline of the show. He conveyed the compliments of the Admiral and the Chief of Staff on the night's activities, and then he nearly killed me with a final request. He wanted reports of proceedings, track charts, ammunition expenditures, signals—in fact, he wanted the life history of our action, and he wanted it as fast as possible. I nipped back for a quick bath and breakfast, and then called all the COs together to give them the good and bad news. We set to work with notebooks and track charts, checking times, courses, positions, and so forth, and began the tedious job of writing the long, boring reports. If we could have jazzed it up by making the reports racy and funny and interesting, it wouldn't have been quite so bad, but the Admiral would probably have taken a dim view of such proceedings. Finally I came to the end of my task, concluding with these words: "This small action was a great uplift to the morale of the 29th MTB Flotilla. As well, we learned a great deal from it, and from what we have learned we hope next time to be more successful." The report went in, and the day's work was done.

On 26 May 1944, the flotilla learned it was to sail to Portsmouth. The Admiral Commanding Dover, Admiral H.D. Pridham-Wippell, sent to Admiralty the following comment on our first action:

> The quick and accurate appreciation by the Senior Officer, Group Baker, enabled him to engage the close escort of the convoy in a spirited five minute action at short range, causing damage to the enemy and materially assisting the withdrawal of Group Able.
>
> This is the first occasion on which a unit of the 29th Flotilla has had an opportunity of taking part in offensive operations in this command and it is regretted that their departure on the 27th May precluded further experience of their keen spirit.

CHAPTER FOUR

THE DAY OF JUDGMENT

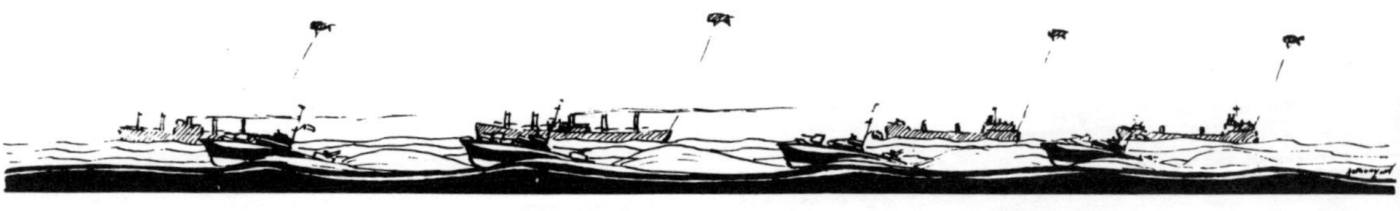

IT WAS IMPOSSIBLE FOR US to leave on the 27th of May, so plans were made to sail on the following day. Pandemonium reigned supreme as the 29th Flotilla packed at maximum speed. In the midst of the confusion I was summoned to the castle in a special car, and John Shand accompanied me. Upon reporting to the Admiral's secretary, I received a large grin. "You're going to die when you see this, but all those white sealed bags—that large pile in the corner—are for your flotilla. They are not to be issued to your officers until a further signal from Admiralty."

So John and I drove back with the Confidential Books (CBs) which the bags contained stacked up to the roof of the car, and with considerable assistance we managed to load them on *459*. We had to store them in a place that could be locked, and this presented a great problem. Finally, in desperation, John, Footsie, and I piled them into the only place that fulfilled security requirements, the wardroom heads, and when the door was finally locked and sealed there wasn't an inch of room to spare. For the remainder of the day we

Right: The author on the bridge of MTB 459, June 1944. (PAC PA144588)

Opposite: The 29th on its way to Normandy. (PAC C127039)

continued packing, and eventually we were able to close the living quarters and hand them over to the Royal Navy. It was obvious to me that the invasion was close at hand.

At 0900 the next day, 28 May, the flotilla departed, waved on its way by the young, feminine charmers of Ramsgate. With the exception of Daddy Bones, who was still refitting at Shoreham, and Bobby Moyse, who had not yet left BP, all the boats were present. Our six craft passed the Dover cliffs and headed through the calm sea toward Dungeness. The sky was cloudless and the air was still, and muggy with heat. As we rounded Dungeness, there appeared what looked at a distance to be a village that had mushroomed overnight. Peering through the binoculars, I saw that it was in reality a congestion of anchored cement blocks, and more were being towed in by four large tugs. On the way by Beachy Head we passed barges and strange pontoon bridges, being towed at caterpillar speed by puffing tugs. My curiosity was aroused, but there was no way it could be satisfied for the time being. Nearing Nab Tower off the Isle of Wight, the unit altered course toward Portsmouth and anchored ships outside the gate vessel on the north side of the Isle of Wight.

Landing craft moved here and there, and saucy little tenders jostled about as we wove our way by the various craft which all seemed to be heading for the one gate vessel. Creeping slowly by the gate vessel so as not to upset the skipper's tea, the 29th piped the Admiral's Flag as it passed Blockhouse, and we received orders to dock on the right of HMS *Vernon,* the RN's anti-submarine training base. Looking around I finally caught sight of *Vernon.* Coastal Force craft buzzed around it thick as flies in a jam pot, and looking to the left, past Haslar Creek and HMS *Hornet,* the Coastal Force establishment, I saw another mass of MTBs at Dolphin pier. It was far different from *459's* last visit, when there had only been five little boats present. We wedged our way into the herd of secured MTBs, and I had to walk over hundreds of craft to get ashore. Perspiration was pouring down my forehead by the time I climbed to the top of the slippery, oily steps and was directed to the Coastal Force Office a few paces away, where sat one, lonely officer. He looked confused and bewildered under the barrage of questions being fired at him by some 20 or 30 officers who were milling around, and he kept repeating the only possible answer: "I can't do anything. There just isn't the space." We were all asking for the same thing, accommodation ashore, but I soon realized that we had no choice but to sleep aboard our little craft. This meant that the CBs would have to be taken out of the heads, and poor Footsie would have to sleep on the deck. When I asked the pathetic RNR officer how we could dispose of the CBs, he replied, "Telephone the CB office at *Hornet* and get in touch with Aunty."

I eventually managed to get hold of a phone to call "Aunty", the CB Officer, and she sounded as if she were in a desperate flap. "For God's sake, get them over here and into the vault. The ones you have are wrong and have been recalled. I'll send a boat over right away."

In no time at all a skimmer came skipping over the water toward my boat, and the pretty little Wren at the helm smiled as she asked, "Are you Lieutenant-Commander Law, Sir?" I replied that I was, and she said, "This is your boat." I called Footsie and some of the crew, and under a scorching sun we proceeded to load the skimmer. By the time all the bags were aboard the CB movers were dripping with sweat. Then Footsie and I went off in the skimmer, bow lifted high in the air with the weight, and before long we had loaded the heavy bags into a cart and were trundling them off to the CB office. When we arrived Aunty was simultaneously carrying on a telephone conversation and talking to about ten people crowded around her desk. Middle-aged, spherical, and robust, sturdy as a battleship, she was well known to Coastal Force personnel, who loved her for her glorious sense of humour.

The CB Office was in utter confusion, and the secret bags were stacked to the ceiling, leaving scarcely enough room in which to turn around. When at last it was my turn to get rid of the annoying CBs, Aunty handed me forms to fill in and sign. The telephone rang constantly, and in the midst of it all Aunty remained calm, though she did say, "My dear, I think I'm going crazy. In fact, I'm sure of it. I've had hundreds of ships return their CBs. What a day!" A few of the bags were too secret to be kept in the office, and she decided that these should be placed in the vault beneath the secretary's office. They were hoisted onto a cart, and Aunty and I, side by side, set out through the base and down to the vault. When we reached the secretary's office I climbed through the trap door, while Aunty, on all fours, puffing and blowing, handed the bags down to me. We were both relieved when the last CB had been placed in bomb-proof safekeeping.

While paying my respects to the Captain of *Hornet,* Captain M. Murray, RN, I put forth our problem of accommodation for the crews and officers. He replied that the situation was grim, but promised that he would see the C-in-C Portsmouth the next day, and as we parted he said, "We'll make you as happy as we can." Back at *Vernon* I found both officers and crews infected by the tingle of excitement and suspense in the air. The great day was not far off!

On the following day I was faced with what seemed like hundreds of problems. At this time the boats possessed only one small hot-plate each and a hot-water urn for coffee, so first of all we somehow had to procure stoves. Admiralty wouldn't play, so I contacted the Canadian Naval Mission Overseas, and they answered with the good news that priority stoves were being sent down. C-in-C Portsmouth ordered the officers of *Vernon* to double up in their cabins to make way for the MTB officers, and needless to say, this move did not earn us much popularity. Once double-deck beds had been installed we all had a bunk, but the 29th's poor base staff drew the leaky old gymnasium, which had to suffice for lack of anything else. The food was not up to much, but it was not difficult to imagine the many problems that must have been encountered in obtaining supplies for such an armada. Sub-Lieutenant A.D. Berlin, RCNVR, my engineer officer (naturally, we called him Irving) arrived from Ramsgate and immediately set to work scrounging spare parts for engines to build up a good reserve for the future. During the day we worked hard preparing our boats, and each evening at 1630 I rang up Peter Scott to get the usual briefing on the night's patrol, which covered 25 miles off the French coast.

Heading the Coastal Force staff was Captain V.P. McLaughlin, RN, and he had the power to push important matters through the correct channels. He was advised by a number of young Coastal Force officers who were up to date on all the tactical aspects. Lieutenant-Commander Peter Scott, MBE, DSC and Bar, RNVR, was his Senior Officer Operations. Among the others who formed this efficient team, which was destined to play an important part in the days to come, were Lieutenants Christopher Dreyer, DSO, DSC, RN; Philip Lee, DSC and Two Bars, RCNR, and Guy Hudson, DSC, RNVR.

One bright morning Peter Scott gave me a ring on the telephone to say that he was sending a car to bring me over to the Old Fort. It was situated on the top of the hills overlooking Portsmouth and commanded a remarkable view of the busy, crowded harbour below. I was taken into the bowels of the earth beneath the Fort to confer with Peter. With him was his famous little perspex-covered chart which gave a complete picture of the Coastal Force area (the English and French coasts). It was truly a mine of information, indicating the Coastal Force patrol routes and German convoy routes, and the minefields were colourfully marked. Wherever Peter went, whether it was to Normandy or to a briefing at some English base, the little chart went with him. After discussing future operations, he took me through the winding corridors and introduced me to Captain McLaughlin. The first question I asked was, "Is there any new light on the phantom W-Boat?" Receiving a negative answer, I then inquired as to whether, in that case, we would regain our torpedo tubes.

"I will give the matter top priority," he replied. "It is essential to have torpedoes for the forthcoming event." The Captain had invited me to stay for lunch, and it was planned that we should meet in the bar where all the naval officers forgathered. After spending a most pleasant day I departed, with high hopes of having our torpedo tubes restored to us.

That evening in the *Vernon* Mess I found Daddy Bones and Bish seated at a gaming table, their stiff collars dispensed with, their shirts open under slackened ties, and their sleeves rolled up in a business-like manner. Bish, his brow wrinkled, looked intense and serious. Chuff-Chuff, with a set grin on his face, was bidding quietly. On his right sat Scobie, wearing an extremely smug expression, and little Howie Hunt with his Churchill-sized cigar slowly blew smoke into the already hazy atmosphere. Dave Killam and Glen Creba concentrated on their cards, neither saying much, and a hawk-eyed Barney Marshall kept close tabs on the bidding. The rest of the 29th's officers had circled around the table to watch the progress of the game. A loud cry from Daddy Bones explained the situation to us: "Stone the crows, Scobie rakes in the chips again." All the while doodlebugs (German rocket bombs) were puffing and sputtering their last gasps overhead. Five seconds later the Mess was shaken violently by a shattering blast . . . but the game continued without pause. Bobby Moyse's voice continued to compete with the chatter of the ack-ack guns as more doodlebugs zoomed above us, and it was not until the wee small hours that the game broke up, with Scobie victorious.

The date was June 4th, 1944, and every highway and by-way leading to Portsmouth harbour was crammed with army tanks, trucks, and heavy equipment of all kinds. In woods and glens, partly concealed by the foliage, more rolling stock was waiting for the signal that would set it in motion. Army police were doing a valiant job of controlling the traffic. Behind closed doors, Daddy Bones and I had been studying the plans for Operation "Neptune", and in the late afternoon I managed to drive along the jammed roads to the Fort for the last time. The car was filled with other Senior Officers on their way to the important briefing, and we all wondered what our individual roles in the invasion

(PAC PA144575)

would be. As we entered the crowded room, we saw Admirals and Captains poring over charts preparatory to briefing us. When the briefing opened we were all tense, straining our ears so that not one word or syllable of instruction should escape us. On the eastern flank of the British Assault Area, the 55th Flotilla, commanded by Lieutenant-Commander Don Bradford, DSO, DSC and Two Bars, RNR, was to maintain eight 'D' class MTBs operational at all times, which left him a reserve of four boats. Then came my turn. Captain Coastal Force regretted that it would be necessary for the 29th Flotilla to maintain 100 percent of its boats operational, which was a tall order since MTBs were of a sensitive and temperamental disposition. Along with the 55th, it was the 29th's

The officers and men of MTB 459. (PAC PA108024)

job to protect the eastern flank of the British Assault Area, and to attack and destroy enemy shipping working from Le Havre. This was one of the toughest assignments received by any of the flotillas, and I felt it a privilege to be given the responsibility. HMS *Scylla,* Admiral Vian's flagship, was to act as mother-ship to all MTBs working under her command. She would also play the part of fighter-control ship, a role similar to that of the Fighter Control in the Air Force. For the first time in history a flagship would control her unit, in this instance consisting of destroyers, frigates, and MTBs, by radar and RT (radio voice transmission) instead of using the wireless, which took too long to vector MTBs onto the enemy. At the close of the briefing all Senior Officers were instructed to make their flotilla officers aware of the plans and to bring all necessary secret charts up to date. We were sealed as of that day, meaning that we had to remain in *Vernon* base. As I drove toward Portsmouth, the prospect of so much work and preparation to be completed in so short a time both excited and worried me. Any overlooked detail could quite easily lead into trouble of unknown proportions. I returned to my flotilla office (shared with three other Senior Officers) and called all my officers for a briefing. When they had all arrived, Footsie and another went to *Hornet* and collected the necessary invasion documents from Aunty. We worked well into the night to bring all the secret navigation matters up to date.

The 5th of June arrived, a dull and miserable day. The wind blew very hard and the sky was overcast with formidable dark clouds. I received a top secret signal; Operation Neptune was on. The knowledge that the long-awaited time had come at last filled me with a strange emotion. As the day wore on the weather deteriorated. An almost incredible variety of ships moved out in an orderly fashion past the Portsmouth gate vessel. Minesweepers appeared off the Normandy coast, and by nightfall the swept channel stretched right across, making the beach-head approaches safe for the hundreds of vessels that were to come. Once the minesweepers had completed their work, destroyers, cruisers, and battleships moved into position to bombard the Normandy coast. Aircraft simultaneously bombed strategic points in Normandy, and were followed by airborne personnel who landed far inland. At the same time, and in spite of the foul weather, shock troops executed the hazardous landing on the beaches. There could be no turning back nor dropping of the curtain on such a huge show just because of the weather. It had to continue according to plan, and to the amazement of the Germans, it did. They were later to say that only fools like the British would think of invading in such weather.

The 29th Flotilla was divided into two striking forces. I was Senior Officer of one of these in *459*, accompanied by Dave Killam in *460*, Charlie Chaffey in *465*, and, at the tail end, Barney Marshall in *466*. The other force was led by Divisional Leader Daddy Bones, while astern of him was Bobby Moyse in *462*, followed by Craig Bishop in *464*, and Glen Creba in *463*. That night of the 5th, Daddy Bones and Bishop were to protect the minesweepers sailing to Normandy against E-boats, and we empathized with him as he set out through the raging seas, winding his way through the endless landing craft before finally slipping out into the angry channel. Choppy seas were very hard on the crews of the

(PAC PA14

little boats. My division of four boats was to leave for Normandy at 1400 on June 6th, and we spent the remainder of that evening making further corrections on our charts. Ships moved ceaselessly throughout the night, all heading for the beaches of Normandy, and thousands of planes droned constantly overhead on their way to join the battle.

6 June 1944—the eyes of the whole world were riveted on Normandy. The wind was still blowing when Bones and Bish returned, sodden and weary after spending a rocky night tossing about and seeing nothing. Their eyes were red-rimmed and their faces caked with salt. Somehow, Deschêsnes, Bones's torpedo man, was still full of energy. He was every place at once, fixing lines and fenders and blasting the younger seamen in broken English. Joe Adams, Bish's Number One, plodded by, his long, white sweater flowing gracefully below his battle jacket. He was extremely worried about the gallons of salt water which he thought he had swallowed during the night at sea.

We finished piling in supplies and ammunition while our new paymaster, Lieutenant Hal Ritchie, issued the stoves and food supplies, and Irving Berlin gave the engines a final check-up. The tiny vessels were loaded to capacity with 2,800 gallons of hundred-octane gasoline for their two-day stay in the Assault Area. At 1400 sharp the colourful pennants went up and the boats moved slowly out into the middle of the harbour, taking up their positions in line-ahead formation. The Number Ones and crews, dressed in their sea-going gear, including the RCN life-jackets with their high collars, lined the fo'c'sle as the Admiral's flag was piped, a ceremony which could under no circumstances be omitted. Then the ships' companies fell out and hastened to action stations, closing up their guns. The four boats, sluggish with their heavy load of gas, yawed back and forth in the line of ships which reached to the horizon. After we had passed through the Solent and rounded Nab Tower at the eastern end of the Isle of Wight, the weather became most unfavourable. Eventually we reached the end of our old course and altered our direction toward Normandy.

During the voyage we passed a most peculiar vessel, which was tossing and bouncing even more than any of the other craft. Closing it we discovered that it was a self-propelled floating kitchen, and it was having an extremely tough time. The kitchen craft closely resembled an overgrown caboose set on a barge, and its many smoking stove-pipes made this unseaworthy Noah's Ark look most out of place battling it out in the mean sea toward Normandy, where it was badly needed. This boat, unique in our experience, quickly faded into the background as our unit moved on, passing in our course other craft far superior to the gallant kitchen ark. These superior craft made up a convoy of merchant ships, manned by valiant officers and men of the Merchant Navy. I have always believed they were truly the Silent Service of the war. Throughout the war merchant ships took part in every major operation, and few people realize the heroic sacrifices made by the seamen who manned them. To every ship wearing a maple leaf, Lovelock the signalman would flash up, "Hello big Canada; this is little Canada," and almost invariably the reply would come back, "Good luck and God speed, little Canada." In spite of the rough weather, we maintained 20 knots, and sometimes Dave's boat would disappear in a cloud of rainbow-coloured spray. Trinity House ships had laid buoys to mark the swept channel, and old Shand's navigation was at its peak. Every buoy or dan-buoy with flag hove in sight at exactly the estimated time. Canadian merchant ships (the Park ships, so called because each was named after a Canadian park) and heavily laden Liberty ships that proudly bore the names of America's great were part of the ceaseless line. The balloons, two streaming from every ship, together looked like a cluster of sparkling diamonds dancing in the stiff breeze.

On and on skimmed the saucy MTBs, creating plumes like the spread tails of haughty peacocks, and leaving wakes like the powerful wings of seagulls. Impudently, our four boats cut across the bows of the slow-moving, cumbersome ships, and in the distance the silhouettes of homeward-bound vessels gradually came into clear sight. These were the ships which had carried shock troops for the initial landing on the now blood-stained beaches of Normandy. They were returning to England, some looking naked without their landing craft. Among them were the three Princes, *Prince David, Prince Henry,* and *Prince Robert,* all famous Canadian ships which had already survived the

Kitchen craft on way to Normandy. (PAC C127024)

invasion of Italy. We signalled "Well done!" Green maple leaves on their funnels were ever-present reminders of home.

On we went, threading our way through the thickening flotillas of landing craft which made it impossible to steer a straight course. *459,* followed by *460, 465,* and *466,* edged toward *Juno,* the typical old Trinity House light vessel which marked the *Juno* area. This red light-ship with its huge white letters was sluggishly heaving and tugging at its anchor with a rather placid look, as if it had been there for many years; it was hard to believe that it had just anchored that morning. Roaring on, I could see other ships lying peacefully at anchor, as if they were back in the quiet Solent. Balloons hovered like a swarm of flies over the mass of shipping, and far beyond them lay the crisp outline of the

The 29th MTB Flotilla en route to Normandy. (PAC PA144576)

Juno, *the Trinity light vessel at the Normandy anchorage. (PAC C126096)*

Normandy coast. The whole crew had come up from below to glimpse the phenomenon, and everyone stared with wide eyes. One of my gunners remarked, "This sure doesn't look war-like."

John was worried lest we shouldn't be able to identify our mother-ship, HMS *Scylla,* in the maze of ships. A rather distinguished-looking destroyer on our starboard side replied to Lovelock's flash that she was approximately six miles northeast of us, and so with direction established we hammered off over the dirty, greenish sea. The wind had increased. We were exceedingly uncomfortable, and cooking became impossible; the rougher the weather, the thicker the sandwiches. Hot coffee was also a problem, because in sipping it more than half poured down one's front as the boat hit yet another mountainous wave. We eventually found *Scylla,* dressed in her cobalt blue and light grey camouflage, nestled among a group of battleships. *Nelson, Warspite,* and others equally renowned, as well as one of the large American battleships, were all booming away together, their projectiles flying inland to give the Army support. As we closed *Scylla,* Lovelock flashed out a signal requesting further orders, and in reply to them Mother *Scylla* soon had four little chicks secured to her stern. A figure with a megaphone appeared high above us. It turned out to be Lieutenant

Opposite: Going home to Scylla, *the mother ship. (PAC C127033)*

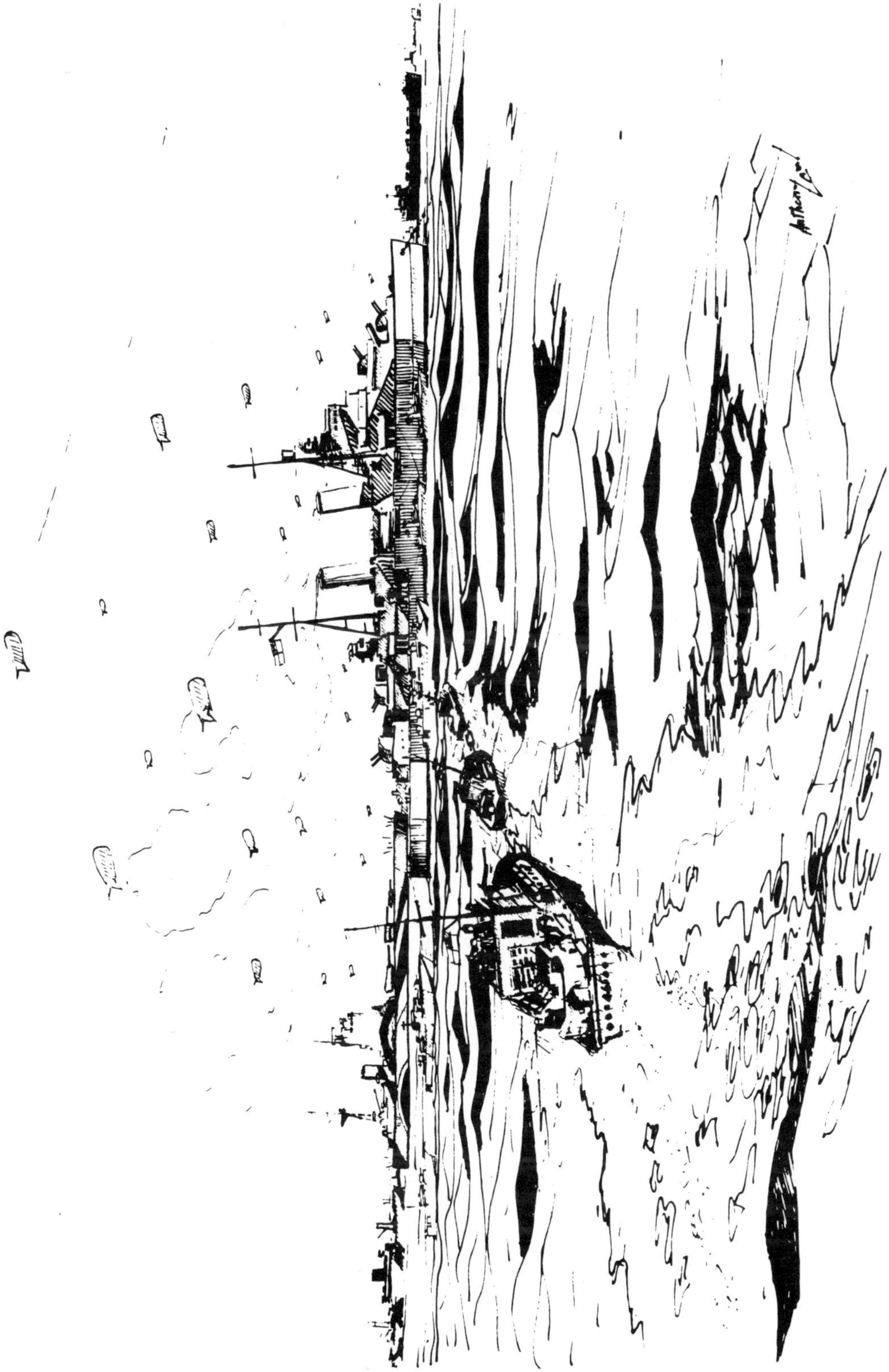

P.N. Edge, DSC, RNVR, the Coastal Force control officer of HMS *Scylla.* With the wind and sea providing stiff competition, old Edge had no easy job briefing us for the patrols of the night's operation. But John, with a notebook, and Footsie and I managed to piece it together well enough to allow us to carry out the first of our nightly patrols in the Assault Area.

Our unit was to patrol three miles northeast of the area, adjusting our position every hour because of the strong tides. Don Bradford and his boats with their distinctive shark-mouth bow markings would be approximately two miles northwest of us, which would place the two groups, backed up by destroyer patrols, about 12 to 14 miles off Cap Le Havre. At the end of the briefing poor Edge had all but lost his voice trying to out-do the howling wind and raging waves, and our little MTBs were bounding on the water like corks. French, my coxswain, was trying to get some warm food together before the patrol began, and old Shand was bellowing out at *460,* passing on the data for the night to Howie Hunt who in turn relayed it to Chuff-Chuff and Marshall. Radio transmission was tested with *Scylla,* whose call sign was ''Bibble''. Ours was ''Slattery'', which was quite a mouthful, especially during a hot engagement with the enemy. When the time came to leave everyone was in black oilskins and life-jackets, and as soon as the order ''Cast off'' was given, our unit steamed off over the rolling sea. Leaving the friendly ships in the Assault Area behind us, we headed northwest to spend our first night alone in the waters off Le Havre. The seas were not kind to us as we lay out in the patrol position, three miles northeast of the Assault Area. Daylight slowly vanished to be replaced by the dark cover of night, and our little band of four tossed restlessly from side to side. Time passed and we adjusted position every hour.

Suddenly the Assault Area awoke as hundreds of tracers were spewed into the air. The cone-shaped fingers of searchlights probed the skies, seeking out enemy aircraft which had begun laying mines and dive-bombing the area. The fantastic quantity of tracer gradually faded from view, and another volley was sent up. It was a dazzling display, and was accompanied by so much roaring and booming and so many violent explosions as to be scarcely credible. Quiet returned as suddenly as it had departed, and once more the night was black and still. The radio transmitter was silent, and even the wind had dropped slightly. Just when the silence was becoming ominous it was broken once more. Don Bradford signalled Bibble (*Scylla*), ''Investigating radar contact.'' Starshells emblazoned the sky, and a battle quickly developed north of us between Don Bradford's flotilla and the enemy. As the tracer sprayed determinedly back and forth, our flotilla hastened to action stations, but before long the uproar ceased,

Opposite: Four MTBs of the 29th Flotilla. (PAC PA141633)

the starshells dimmed out, and I could see Bradford's boats coming down toward us. He passed about 200 yards ahead of our flotilla, proceeding on a southerly course, and I decided that since we had had a quiet night we would track on astern of him.

Sighting six enemy silhouettes to the northeast, and noticing that Bradford was doing nothing about them. I broke off and headed in that direction, radioing to Dave, Chuff-Chuff, and Barney, "Maximum speed; we're going in to attack." As our boats sped over the sea in battle formation, I returned the radio to Footsie, telling him to make Bibble aware of our intentions. The order was to illuminate, and the six R-Boats stood out clearly in the red glare provided by our angry pom-poms. Simpson, the radar operator, reported the bearing and the range, which was now closing rapidly. The R-Boats were on an easterly course in line-ahead, and we were quickly catching up abeam of them.

At 700 yards all four of our boats opened up with intense, concentrated fire, and we closed in to 150 yards. It was a furious battle. The tracer, thick and penetrating, hit *459* in several places, including the chart-house, thus putting the QH (electronic navigational aid) set out of action. John Shand, shaken by the explosion, pulled aside the curtain and looked up to the bridge to see what was going on. He was confronted by three pairs of glassy, frightened eyes. Footsie, the coxswain, and I had also been shaken by the force of that

last resounding Oerlikon shell. Bushfield, the Number Two on our pom-pom, had sustained a serious wound, but he continued feeding his gun despite his pain. In *466,* Barney's two gunners, Wright and Howarth, had also been hit. All four of our boats had suffered damage or casualties at the hands of the enemy. But we had managed to blow up and sink one R-Boat, and in another a fire broke out which, unfortunately, was shortly extinguished.

As a climax to the battle, mines suddenly began to explode around the R-Boats and ourselves, and I soon realized that we were in the British mine-field known as the Area Scollops a few miles off Le Havre. After our ten-minute engagement at close range, I was forced to disengage, making a smoke-screen as we steamed northward out of the dangerous mine-field, which had doubtless frightened the wits out of the enemy as well as out of me. Bushfield was suffering extreme pain by this time, so Footsie gave him morphine and rendered first aid. The gunner was then carried gently down to the coxswain's cabin by Footsie and other members of the crew, who made him as comfortable as possible.

When all boats arrived back on original patrol positions, we closed to discuss damages and casualties. McAulley, the wireless operator, with a cigarette dangling from the corner of his mouth and his tin hat pushed far back on his head, banged out a coded message to *Scylla,* giving her a brief outline of our engagement with the six R-Boats.

The cold dawn broke over a sea still capped with ruffled foam. Overhead the clouds scurried briskly by. It was another miserable day for MTBs. The only thing which seemed to be in our favour was the clock, which, having moved around to 0500, allowed us to leave the patrol. The four little boats pounded home to Mother *Scylla,* relieved to see her once again. But before we could relax there was a problem to be faced. Casualties had to be landed, but with the breaking seas threatening to crash us against her sides it was difficult to get alongside *Scylla.* Though we might have accomplished this feat, we learned that *Scylla's* sick bay was already filled beyond what it could handle. The doctor directed us to the hospital ship which was lying inshore off *Scylla.* So Chuff-Chuff and Dave tied up astern of a destroyer while Barney and I set off toward the white ship, but we reached her only to find that she was also crowded to capacity. Our hearts fell, and hungry and tired we set off in search of the LST which the mercy ship had suggested. There were hundreds of LSTs, all looking alike under the grey, sullen sky, and after a desperate search we finally came alongside a British destroyer. The destroyer's doctor came aboard to see what could be done for our wounded, but with no operating equipment

Opposite: The battle with six R-Boats off Le Havre, 6/7 June 1944. (PAC C127038)

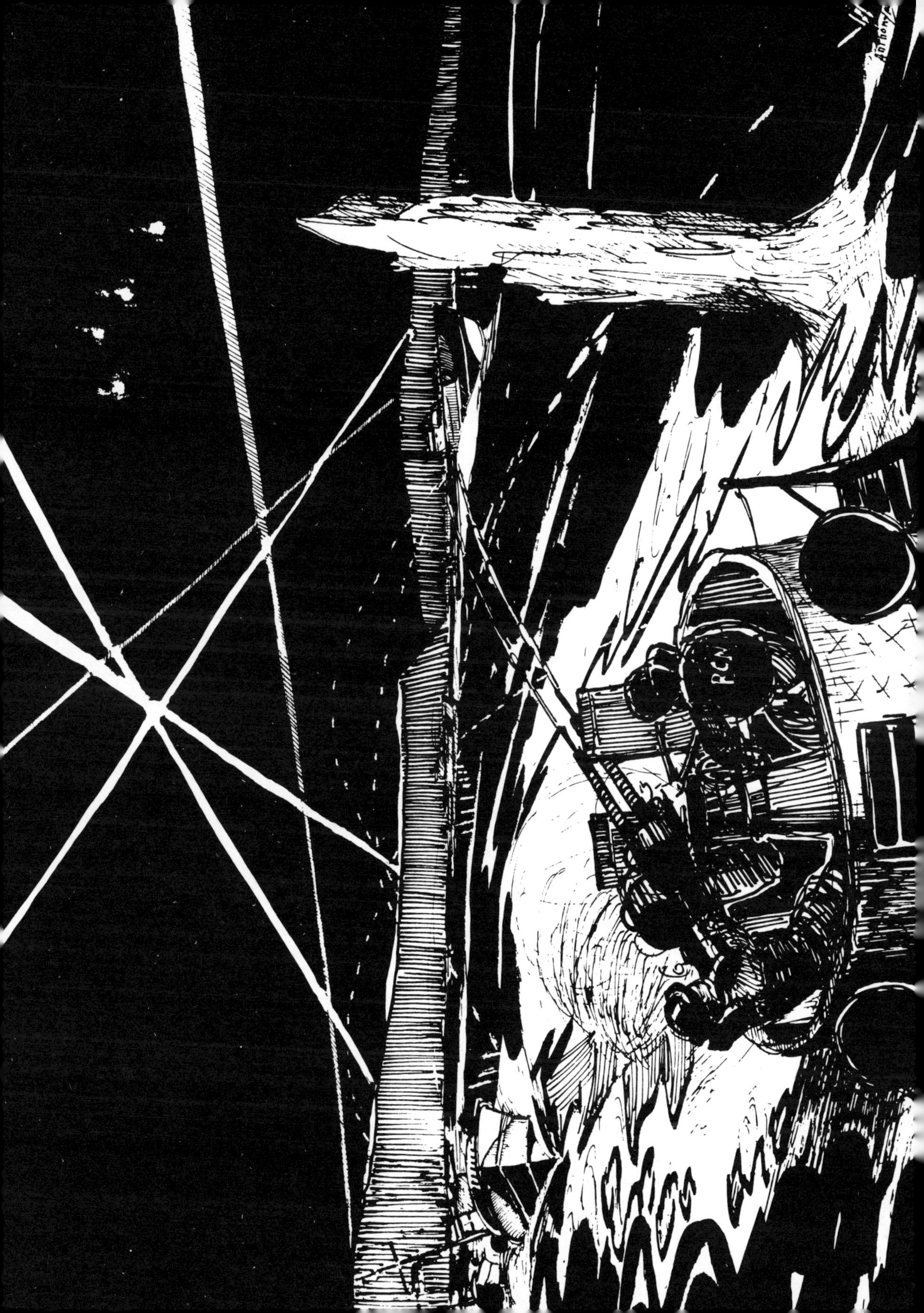
RCN

his aid was limited. On the doctor's request, one of the destroyer's signalmen agreed to locate the elusive LST-turned-hospital-ship. It took a whole hour for our one hope to be found, after which we thanked the destroyer, set out for the LST, and secured with great difficulty to her port side. For a moment we feared that it would be impossible to get our wounded aboard the towering ship, but a rope was lowered and attached to the stretcher, after which old Bushfield, feeling extremely seedy by this time, was hauled carefully aboard. *466* went through the same slow procedure, and Wright and Howarth were soon safely inside the LST. Our task at last accomplished, we found a nice, fat merchant ship, which looked laden with supplies. Since she would be unlikely to move for a day or so, we made fast to her. I was so tired that I dropped into my bunk already dreaming. John quickly occupied the upper bunk, and poor Footsie had to be satisfied with a mattress laid on the deck . . . but he was so weary he didn't care. *466* secured astern, and its occupants also grasped the opportunity for sleep.

Waking from a deep slumber, I slid out of the bunk and climbed to the upper deck for a breath of fresh air and a cigarette. I was just taking a long leisurely drag when I noticed *Scylla* on our starboard quarter flashing us up, and I yelled down the voice-pipe for Lovelock. He looked a pathetic little figure, climbing up the ladder with both eyes clamped shut. Automatically he picked up the Aldis light and started flashing . . . in the wrong direction. I tapped him gently and pointed over his shoulder, whereupon he turned round and continued to flash. Gradually his eyes opened and he more or less came to life. It took only a few seconds for him to realize that we were being directed "Come alongside". There was no rest for the weary.

"Start up," I yelled down the voice-pipe, and Dawson nipped up on the deck and was in the engine-room in a flash. I could see old Barney, astern of me in *466*, wiping the sleep out of his eyes, looking like Humphrey Bogart behind his day-old black beard. The sun was out, the wind had dropped, and it was good to be alive. We cast off and moved slowly in the direction of the mother-ship. Reaching her, we tied up, well cushioned by fenders, and were greeted by Lieutenant Edge, who asked us for a short report of the night's activities. He also told us that Admiral Vian, who was very pleased with what had gone on, wished to meet us on *Scylla's* bridge.

The four COs led by Edge made way to the bridge where Admiral Vian was standing, his binoculars ready for use. Vian, a tall, well built man, was clothed in battledress and wore his hat at a rakish angle. Our introduction to him was rudely interrupted by a devil-may-care German tank which had broken through the Army lines and rolled down to the edge of the beach. Impudently it started to fire at the flagship, *Scylla,* and the Admiral remarked, "What an insolent fellow. I admire his courage." Its triumph was short-lived, for two

(PAC PA136831)

British tanks soon roared down beside it to take the German crew prisoner. In the meantime, a *Stuka* had droned in and dive-bombed an ammunition dump, which went up with a bang, leaving masses of black smoke billowing into the sky. This was the background for our introduction to Admiral Vian. After a brief conversation we saluted and returned to our boats. Edge had informed us that we were free till 1700, when we would have the usual natter, so in the meantime the four MTBs bubbled off to a nice soft spot behind a battleship. After having a bite to eat and a slight wash-up, I climbed back into my good old bunk and had another snooze, which, unfortunately, was constantly interrupted by dreams of actions, snores from below, and the cracking of guns as the battleships and cruisers kept up their barrage. In this manner the day passed quickly, and at 1700 the four of us from the 29th joined others in *Scylla's* briefing room to scribble the dispositions for the night's work in our notebooks. A civilian appeared on the scene carrying rolls of charts under his arm, which in due course he unfurled on the chart table. He was the weatherman, and he informed us in sonorous tones that these charts, indicating the high pressures and low pressures, promised us a calm and beautiful night.

Before going back to my boat I asked one of the hundreds of war correspondents aboard *Scylla* how the Army was doing in their push, and he replied, "Haven't the vaguest idea. Better go back to England and read a newspaper." Hell of a help he was!

One half-hour later we had arrived at our allotted position, which was practically the same one we had taken up on the 6th and 7th of June. Tonight, the 7th and 8th, only God knew what was in store for us. Contrary to the little weatherman's predictions, the wind grew more and more violent. I guess he must have read his charts upside down. The destroyers were nattering over the RT to *Scylla,* and in return being vectored over the ocean to play frustrating games with ironized MacGoffoneys. While they floodlit the skies with pretty starshells, we continued to adjust our positions every hour on the dot. A nasty German aircraft dropped a huge mine just ahead of us, and the splash as it fell into the sea so jangled our nerves that we moved off to a safer zone.

In this position, three miles off the Assault Area, we got a call from *Scylla,* "Hello Slattery; hello Slattery. Vector, 280°, seven miles, over."

"Slattery, roger out."

Urged on by the excitement, the engines coughed and spluttered into life, and a phosphorescent wake illuminated our herringbone pattern as the four boats sped over the sea at top speed. Since we were no longer carrying the large quantities of gasoline with which we had started the operation, our speed was markedly increased and the craft was much easier to handle. Simpson, with his magic eye, was searching the dark horizon for radar contacts, but we arrived at our positions only to find it barren of the enemy. *Scylla* signalled, "Negative how-how. Vector, Vector [back to your original position]."

As we were carrying out Bibble's instructions, Simpson suddenly piped up, "Enemy aircraft must be dropping tinsel." Planes droning above quickly confirmed this report. We continued meandering along, till starshells, which seemed to come from the direction of our destroyer patrol, suddenly broke over us. The radar had started to work, and Simpson picked up two echoes at about 6,000 yards. As the sods continued to put starshells over our heads, all four of us switched on fighting lights to indicate that we were friendly. Still we were illuminated, and the range had closed to 5,000 yards. Our little unit challenged, but even though we received no reply, I was still convinced that we were dealing with friends. Then, at 4,800 yards, the bullies opened fire on us.

Footsie put in a desperate call to *Scylla,* "Hello Pibble or Bibble or whatever your name is; this is Slattery. Tell your destroyers to stop shooting at us. Over."

"Hello Slattery. This is Bibble. Wait," came the answer.

The range was now 4,000 yards, and the sky was cluttered with starshells while other shells from heavy-calibre guns crashed about us, sending up tall towers of spray. Since the 29th had done everything possible to identify itself, we had to conclude that we were facing enemy destroyers. Increasing speed to 25 knots, our four midget-sized boats burst into action. We opened fire with the pom-poms, forgetful of the fact that some of the guns were loaded with 14 pom-pom starshells, which roared out and landed on the decks of the German destroyers, lighting them up like Christmas trees. The destroyers were a couple of the *Möwe* class, old, but still formidable. Soon the real stuff came out, and the scarlet glow of red-hot rivets appeared on the enemy's hulls. The range, now 500 yards, continued to close.

As the battle reached its peak, *Scylla* broke in on the RT, "Hello Slattery; this is Bibble. They are two German destroyers and we cannot help. Over."

Footsie retorted, "Hello Bibble. You said it. Over," and there was so much zest in the message that one would have supposed he was broadcasting a hockey match. We all turned away together, *459* making smoke to cover the other three, and the little vessels disengaged at maximum speed. The boost needle had gone twice around the boost dial. We travelled in Order 1, but the shells fell so close to Chuff-Chuff that Barney, sure that Chuffy was hit, broke line to avoid running over the wreckage. Chuff-Chuff came through the spray, his decks streaming water from the shower, and I'm certain his face was grey at that moment.

John yelled up to the coxswain, "What course are you steering?"

"Northeast, Sir," French replied.

"For God's sake, you're heading straight for Le Havre!"

The destroyers were hot on our tails, shooting through the smokescreen. "Port wheel, coxswain," I ordered, and it seemed to take an eternity for the unit to swing gradually around . . . north . . . northwest . . . and, accompanied by a sigh of relief, south, toward the good old Assault Area. The battle was over! We hadn't done too badly, considering that *459* didn't have Bushfield and that *466* was short two gunners. But our greatest misfortune, which assumed almost tragic proportions, was that we had had no torpedoes and carried only those little depth charges. With torpedoes we might have been able to give those boys their money's worth. Don Bradford's flotilla did have a go with torpedoes at the two *Möwes*, but it was hard to say whether or not he got a hit.

By this time the clock had rolled around to 0330 and the east was tinged with a dull, greyish light, which would gradually grow brighter as the sun stuck

Disengaging after battle with two enemy destroyers, 7/8 June 1944. (PAC C127025)

its nose above the cliffs of Le Havre. By 0500 our four MTBs had ploughed their way back to dear old Mother *Scylla,* a salty spray deluging the bridges every foot of the way. Lieutenant Edge, waiting on the upper deck of the cruiser, was anxious to learn what damage we had inflicted upon the enemy. Although we had observed many hits, it seemed unlikely that we had caused any severe damage and no doubt we had merely made the night a bit unpleasant for them.

The boats tied up astern once more. Though we were weary and wet there still remained a spark of undampened humour. Lovelock, sighting a smart-looking destroyer sporting a maple leaf, flashed her up, "Hello big Canada; this is little Canada."

Instead of the usual reply, he got, "Hello little Canada. This is Admiral Nelles. Will be coming aboard to visit you at 0800." The crew, exhausted after their two-day sojourn in the Assault Area, nevertheless pulled themselves together and tried to square off the ship and tidy her up a bit. They had had but little sleep, and food picked up only at odd moments, for it had been impossible to have a proper hot meal in that rough weather. Tossed about by the rolling waves, the four MTBs tugged violently at their lines, and the hundred-octane gasoline rumbled back and forth in the petrol tanks. But despite it all, the ships' companies managed to put in a spot of sleep before 0800.

The time passed far too quickly, and at the appointed hour Admiral Percy Nelles, in the Admiral's barge belonging to *Scylla,* made two attempts to come alongside. One minute the tiny craft would soar above us atop a mighty wave, and the next it would drop far below, threatening to crash alongside. On the second attempt the Admiral jumped, and as we grabbed his arms Lovelock piped him aboard. Admiral Nelles spoke to the crews and officers, congratulating them on the two actions, and then accepted our offer of some hot chocolate. The chocolate was almost as thick as molasses, but it was the best *459* could do, as the weather was far too rough for an MTB to attempt fancy cooking. Due to circumstances beyond our control, the wardroom was untidy and draped with wet clothes, but the Admiral didn't seem to mind, and we had a long conversation. Before departing he asked if we would take him back to Portsmouth, and naturally I replied that we should be delighted.

Attaining the deck of his small barge with one long leap, Admiral Nelles was on his way to keep his appointment with Admiral Vian. The other three boats, *460, 465,* and *466,* were ordered to return to Portsmouth, while *459,* which would remain in the Assault Area until the afternoon, made fast alongside HMCS *Algonquin.* Lieutenant-Commander "Debby" Piers was the commanding officer of this noble ship, and since it was his birthday he very kindly invited John, Footsie, and myself aboard to dine. The meal was excellent, and later there were movies aboard his ship for *459's* crew. We were treated like kings.

Returning from his tour in the Assault Area, Admiral Nelles, his Flag Lieutenant, and Lieutenant-Commander G.F. Tod, RCNVR, came aboard *459.* The engines burst into noisy life, lines were let go, and we moved gently away, leaving the friendly destroyer to merge into an horizon dotted with many ships. With just enough gasoline aboard to reach Portsmouth, the MTB was light and fast, and the Admiral sat on the small seat on the bridge with a lovely, fresh breeze blowing in his face. Skimming along at 35 knots, we met Daddy Bones heading for the Assault Area with only two of his ships astern, and Lovelock flashed him the message, "Good luck; you'll need it." Within a few more hours we had tied up alongside the other three MTBs of the 29th. Admiral Nelles's Wren driver was invited aboard, and we all relaxed in the wardroom to have a pleasant discussion and partake of some Amontillado sherry. A short while later, the Admiral thanked us for his enjoyable trip, and we piped him over the side.

All four boats were flying a variety of pennants from their yardarms, denoting the individual defects which had need of repair. Shipwrights and engineers were already hard at work on the other three craft, and in short order *459* was besieged by workers banging patches over her battle scars. The highest tribute should be paid to all those who worked non-stop, night and day, to keep the boats operational. There was no glory attached to their arduous tasks, and they received but small thanks or appreciation. Irving Berlin and his little band of base staff worked for 48 hours without pause and they had borne as great a strain as the sea-going crews. If it hadn't been for their great work, our ships could never have left the jetty.

Meanwhile, on the night of 8-9 June, Daddy Bones in *461,* Bobby Moyse in *462,* and Glen Creba in *463* had all reached *Scylla* in the Assault Area. They made fast alongside the mother-ship and were briefed by Lieutenant Edge. The same weatherman, bearing his numerous charts, announced in his reassuring manner that the weather would be beautiful, with neither a puff of wind nor a ripple upon the water. This made the unsuspecting Daddy Bones, Moyse, and Creba very happy. After the briefing the boats were off on the patrol, three miles north of the Assault Area, and the light faded and blackness fell.

The night opened with the usual extravaganza. Searchlights and flak filled the sky, aeroplanes droned overhead as they dropped their mines, and natter floated over the RT from MacGoffoney-chasing destroyers. At 2339 the three MTBs lay wallowing in the heavy seas, which had been whipped into a tantrum by the angry winds. The weather simply refused to co-operate with the weatherman. Two very small, fast boats passed them on a westerly course, and one jaunty fellow passed 25 yards astern of Creba, greeting him with a burst from his light-calibre machine-guns. The three MTBs were jolted to action stations, and engines started up one after another until they were all roaring in harmony. The unit shoved off with revs pushed up to maximum, but they were soon outdistanced by the swift craft which continued to pursue their westerly course. Sub-Lieutenant I.W. Robertson, Daddy Bones's Third Officer, informed *Scylla* of their escapade, and Bones and his little band of pirates returned to patrol position. Everything was quiet until 0106, when *Scylla* vectored the group onto a suspicious echo in the direction of Cap d'Antifer. The unit sped toward the Cape, but could not catch up with the craft trying to sneak into the Le Havre harbour, so *Scylla* ordered her charges to stop.

(PAC PA137023)

No sooner had the engines been cut than *Scylla* picked up another echo. Almost immediately a powerful German starshell burst overhead, displaying the three boats standing naked against the black background. The same two wicked *Möwe* class destroyers were out again. Daddy Bones and Company moved off to shadow the enemy and give radar reports to the control ship. The fun and games began as the destroyers began to fire with all their armament. The MTB unit returned the fire—somewhat like a mouse spitting in a tiger's eye—but they managed to get in some good punches, many hits being observed. Meanwhile they continued to move gallantly forward, managing to close to 400 yards (which is damned close). The battle then became so furious that they were forced to disengage under the welcome cover of smoke. The boats were slightly damaged, but quickly caught their breath and moved off to their old patrol route. But it was a sad night for the 29th. Frederick T. Armstrong, one of the crewmen of MTB *464,* had been instantly killed by a direct hit. The hearts of Bish and his crew were heavy as they mourned the loss of their close comrade.

The night of 9-10 June proved to be the first uneventful night the unit had encountered for some time. Of course the Assault Area put on its usual fireworks display, enemy aircraft dropped mines throughout the region, and destroyers nattered to each other all night, but dawn found the four MTBs rocking undisturbed in the rhythmic swell, glowing warmly in the early light. Silence was broken as the engines began to warm up, and the boats moved slowly in the direction of the control ship. Soon afterward they were headed toward Portsmouth, where they would have a 48-hour refit and the crews would get a good sleep.

On the night of 10-11 June, *459, 460, 465,* and *466* were back in the Assault Area. Very little happened, other than the odd mine being dropped and dive bombers shaking up the area. We spent the night being vectored over the seas chasing false echoes. The next night passed in a similar manner. The Assault Area was involved with enemy action, but we were spared trouble by the destroyers which patrolled to and fro ahead of us. Our group was soon on its way home again, and once more we met Daddy Bones with his unit in mid-channel as he went to replace us.

Daddy Bones and I saw very little of each other those days, but we managed to communicate by means of a little blue book which sat in the drawer of the desk in the Flotilla Office. In it were listed all the flotilla's problems, as well as chit-chat on the latest gossip and the choicer bits of Portsmouth scandal. This book also allowed us to keep track of business which could not be completed before the unit sailed, and it helped us to more easily solve the difficulties confronting the flotilla. In early June one of our difficulties was solved: all our craft were refitted with the torpedo tubes.

On the evening of 12 June, Daddy Bones found himself at the usual briefing, and this time Bish was with him, strengthening the unit to four boats. The weatherman delivered his forecast, which was the same as usual, and the officers climbed aboard their ships and headed out toward the terrifying battle-ground to wait for *Scylla* to pick out the foe. Sure enough, out came the same two enemy destroyers. This time, though, *Scylla* used the four MTBs as decoys while she manoeuvred her destroyers into position, in the hope of giving the Germans a thrashing.

The four saucy MTBs, unaware that they were being used as bait, were all ready for Bish to move in for a torpedo attack. A brief engagement ensued, but

(PAC PA144579)

the little boats were forced to disengage in a blanket of smoke, with orders to cease smoke after having reached a respectable distance. Suddenly, a dive bomber attacked the phosphorescent wake of *461,* striking so close to her that the blast shot all the gas out of the carburetors, causing the engine to stop instantly. When she had recovered from the shock, *461* got her engines going and resumed her patrol position. Poor old Bish was very disappointed because he hadn't been able to fire his lovely new torpedoes at the two destroyers. Meanwhile, the two British destroyers had manoeuvred into position and were trying to coax the enemy to give battle, but the German ships fled quickly to the protection of Le Havre harbour.

The four MTBs later rejoined *Scylla.* After giving a rough picture of the night's encounter, they tied up astern for the day. Daddy Bones and his clan were finally able to rest quietly, and they had a fast game of bridge to break the monotony of the afternoon. The night was peaceful too, broken only by enemy dive bombers indiscriminately dropping the usual ration of mines, and the unit had to do nothing but adjust its position hourly. As usual, the destroyers carried on a ceaseless natter over the RT, though they were shushed from time to time by Mother *Scylla.* The night passed slowly, but eventually the boats left the area, reported to the control ship, and then set sail for home.

CHAPTER FIVE

SHOWING THE STRAIN

ON 15 JUNE 1944, OUR FOUR BOATS—*459, 460, 465,* and *466*—were once more off the Normandy beaches. We spent two days chasing ironized MacGoffoneys and getting ourselves diced up by the Le Havre shore batteries, an extremely uncomfortable experience, especially when it coincided with dodging the odd floating mine. By this time the members of the 29th Flotilla had become expert scroungers, and I particularly remember the occasion when Barney Marshall was badly in need of bread and water. Taking a step in the right direction, he chose as his victim the biggest and fattest ship in the area, none other than the battleship HMS *Nelson. Nelson* hob-nobbed only with the dignitaries, tolerating nothing less than a destroyer, and MTBs to her probably represented the lowest form of marine life. Nevertheless, *466,* devoid of class-consciousness, sailed up to her, and the audacious Barney hailed a dignified Brass Hat with, "Can you let us have some water?"

The BH peered down from the heights and replied in stentorian tones, "Don't you youngsters realize that we have to make our own water aboard this ship?"

Barney, not easily put off, continued to plead in a tear-choked voice. "We're desperate! Can't you let us have just a little?"

The stately Senior Officer, no doubt touched by Barney's earnest manner, finally relented. "Well, I can only let you have 800 gallons."

Poor Barney gulped, opened and closed his mouth, and gulped again. Finally he managed to regain his power of speech, and answered, "Good Lord, Sir, 800 is too much. Our tanks can only take 45 gallons."

Mingled with deep chuckles, the reply from the Senior Officer came down. "Why didn't you tell me that in the first place?"

While the water was being taken aboard *466,* Barney, still glowing with confidence from his initial success, yelled up to another of *Nelson's* Senior Officers who had appeared, standing miles above him. "Could you please let us have some bread?"

"Yes. Come on up and get it."

Barney gazed doubtfully up the ship's side, which seemed the equivalent of the Empire State Building. But never at a loss for words, he asked innocently, "What do you want me to do, wait till the tide comes up?" With a smile, the Senior Officer arranged to have the bread thrown down to *466.* Barney, his problems taken care of, departed with the pleasant knowledge that he had scrounged off one of the biggest battleships in the Royal Navy.

The time passed, and on 16 June we returned to Portsmouth for a refit. Daddy Bones replaced us, returning on the 18th with a drab tale of inactivity off the Normandy coast. By this time 50 percent of the MTBs had regained their torpedo tubes, and the 29th Canadian Flotilla was now a powerful unit

Opposite: MTBs lying out on patrol. (PAC C127021)

capable of attacking convoys and dealing severely with them. But, as fate would have it, just when most of the boats had been fitted with their fangs, it became increasingly difficult to find targets. Ever since the bombing of Le Havre, which had burned unceasingly for two days, the German Navy had neither put to sea offensively nor tried to sneak convoys into Le Havre harbour. The battle for Caen was raging fiercely and the beautiful French city had been reduced to a rubble-strewn skeleton. The fighting was bloody and bitter, and the British and Canadian troops were paying a tremendous price for every yard they gained.

460 was suffering from an acute attack of engine and propeller trouble, so Dave Killam had not sailed with us, but *459, 465,* and *466* wearily patrolled their beat throughout the nasty, windy night. On the morning of 19 June we returned to *Scylla,* wet and worn, and informed her that we would take shelter behind "Gooseberry", a breakwater of old merchant ships which had been sunk in a semi-circle opposite Port aux Courseulles. About a mile and a half from the beach at the farthest points, Gooseberry afforded excellent shelter to small

vessels such as personnel landing craft and MTBs. The three boats poked their way through the thick mass of small craft and secured alongside one of the sunken merchant ships. It was cosy and friendly there, and among our neighbours we recognized our old pal the floating kitchen. Opposite Arromanches, about three miles south of us, I spotted the familiar cement blocks, still being towed by the patient, puffing tugs. I realized that they were to be sunk as a breakwater, and my long-aroused curiosity was finally satisfied. It was no easy task to get the cement blocks into place, continually hampered by the shifting waves, but the significance of this gigantic engineering feat was instantly apparent. These huge cement structures, which brilliant strategists had once concentrated off Dungeness to decoy the enemy into expecting an invasion by way of Dunkirk, were being pieced together to form a harbour, complete with breakwater and floating piers.

All that morning the tempo of the wind increased, and by afternoon it had developed into a strong gale which sent great, grey clouds scudding along beneath an overcast sky. The seas were smothered by angry spume, and ships tugged resentfully at their anchors. The cocky tugs which had been towing the breakwater sections lost their complacent attitude and began to look frightened when their tow-lines broke and the usual complications ensued. We MTBs were comparatively safe and snug, riding comfortably in the cosy harbour of Gooseberry even though the wind had reached hurricane force. As the storm raged on we became aware of a large repair ship drifting down toward the sunken ships which formed our breakwater. Her engines had broken down, her two anchors were dragging on the sandy bottom, and when one of the tiny tugs tried to take her in tow, the line became wrapped under the helpless ship's propeller. What a mess! In the midst of the excitement *Scylla* sent us a signal via one of Gooseberry's ships, which served as a signal station, telling us that all operations were cancelled due to the heavy gales and ordering us to remain in our shelter. The tide continued to rise, and the sea, now blanketed by white caps, tossed tumultously. The shrieking wind caught the spray in its angry fists and in a frenzy threw it down again, while the powerful waves crashed against the sunken line of ships, knocking them together stem to bow. The American tugs were busy towing in little boats that had fallen helpless in the face of the storm. Then the waves came crashing over the merchant ships to which we were secured, and the spray thundered down on the decks of the MTBs, which seemed to have grown smaller during the furious onslaught.

Opposite: Two boats of the 29th alongside one of the sunken "Gooseberry" merchant ships. 465 is the inboard boat. Both have been refitted with their torpedo tubes. (PAC PA108025)

Our position was becoming precarious, and although all lines had been doubled the three boats tugged at them threateningly as they elevatored up the mountains of water and then dived dizzily into the pits between the huge rolling waves. The wear and tear of crashing together with other boats and ships was beginning to tell on our fenders. The sea struggled desperately to prove that it was the master of all men, and the seriousness of our plight loomed larger with the passing of each minute. The tide was still sweeping in, and before long the upper-deck cabins of Gooseberry's antiquated ships were flooded. Their occupants, the Marines who ran the personnel landing-craft, were forced to take to their boats and make for the narrow entrance to Port aux Courseulles. By driving these adversaries from their homes, it seemed that the sea had won the first round in the championship fight.

Our fenders had long since expended themselves, and in desperation Chuff-Chuff, Barney, and I, working alongside the crews, began making replacements for them by chopping up huge cables belonging to one of the tomb-like merchant ships. The wind whined and whistled menacingly through the ghost ship. Rigging squeaked and iron doors slammed, echoing eerily in our ears. Some of the mooring lines had parted, and these too had to be hastily repaired. My rubbing strakes had also been carried away by the merciless waves. Soon darkness fell over the area, intensifying the roaring of the sea and the howling of the wind. As if we hadn't enough trouble, a German aircraft swooped low overhead and dropped a bomb not far off. Guns opened up from all directions, following the beams of the searchlight.

At this point, Chuff-Chuff, Barney, and I got together and decided that the complete company of each ship should take turns in carrying out a watch on the upper decks of all three boats. *459* was to take the first four hours, followed by *465*, who would be relieved by *466*. In this way we should all get an opportunity to sleep. During our watch the coxswain and I travelled from ship to ship checking on lines and fenders, while John and Footsie helped the crew repair the ones that were damaged. The wind was blowing even more fiercely and the tide was still rising. The gigantic waves were now flinging themselves across the old merchant ship, tearing at her with frenzied fingers and smashing into a thousand splinters the wooden rafts fitted on the port and starboard sides of her rigging. Throughout the night the struggle continued, but toward morning the tide began to drop, and once again the merchant ships afforded us shelter from the breaking waves. When morning came the sun pierced holes in the clouds and accentuated the whiteness of the sea horses.

The barrage balloons yawed back and forth, occasionally disappearing altogether into the clouds, and the weather, instead of improving, grew worse. A motor gun boat flashed us the message, "You are to proceed into Port aux Courseulles for shelter." As soon as I had given the order to start up, John,

Storm at the Gooseberry, Normandy. (PAC C127022)

Barney, Chuff-Chuff, and myself studied in detail the entrance to this port. It was a dangerously difficult entrance because the shallow waters were flanked by hundreds of steel obstructions, placed there by the enemy in order to pierce holes in any craft that might attempt a landing on the beach. After a short consultation I decided to give a running commentary over the RT as we approached the entrance.

The boats moved off into the heavy, breaking seas toward the narrow opening, and soon the wicked-looking steel prongs on either side of the harbour were plainly visible. Landing craft which had been caught on those devilish entanglements were being bashed to pieces by the gigantic rollers, and wreckage from vessels of every sort was piled along the beaches as far as the eye could see. As we approached the shore the waves lifted us high into the air and then dropped us with a shuddering thud. Each passing minute brought *459* closer to the steel obstructions at the mouth of the harbour, which was only a hundred feet wide. The coxswain was at the wheel, snapping it quickly from port to starboard to check the boat from swinging broadside into the breaking waves. We eased slowly through the entrance, and sighed with relief when we reached the quiet waters inside. While *459* wedged her way through the mass of landing craft I communicated with Chuff-Chuff and Barney, warning them of the obstructions on the port side of the dangerous entrance. At last they too were safely through, and my worries were over as the two MTBs caught up with me and followed close astern. Together we travelled 200 yards upstream, passed through the little gates at the end of the harbour, and entered the tidal basin. At high tide these gates would be closed and the MTBs would be left sitting in a basin scarcely bigger than a large duck pond.

Dotting the shores around us were the once-charming but now battered cottages of the Norman peasants, and to the right of us two-armed steam shovels were dredging the harbour to maintain the six-foot depth of water necessary to float MTBs and Motor Launches. We moved to the port side of the basin and secured to the primitive pier. The two other boats secured alongside MTB *459*. Now we didn't care how furiously the wind blew; our boats were safe in the cosy French harbour. Many of us were looking forward to setting foot for the first time on French soil.

I had heard that no one was to be allowed ashore, but taking into consideration the cramped quarters in the boats I permitted a few of the men to walk as far as the village of Courseulles to stretch their legs. In short order a pathetic little figure accompanied by two red-capped MPs was back, and I was politely informed that we all had to remain on board the MTBs. I immediately stormed off to find the Naval Officer in Charge, and soon located him in a beautiful, typically French villa. All the surrounding buildings bore battle scars, but nothing had marred the simple and lovely architecture of this one. I was

Sheltered at Port aux Courseulles. (PAC C127029)

escorted into the presence of the NOIC, who quite abruptly informed me that the order must stand. When I stressed the difficulty of adequate exercise on the small MTBs, he tried to appease me by saying that the crews could walk up and down the beach opposite the boats. I could just picture the men of the 29th having their early morning PT walk beside the boats; my, wouldn't they find it exciting! Before I left, the NOIC, in a casual manner, informed me that the wind would continue to blow Force 9 or 10—hurricane force—for at least two more days.

Arriving back at the boats, I found my crews listening to a small French lad, who was telling them stories of the German occupation. Apparently, anyone who refused to work for the Germans had received no food. McAulley, the telegraphist, his French-Canadian accent slightly tinged with an Irish brogue, was interpreting the conversation for the rest of his chums. The ship's company invited the boy aboard for a really good lunch, and the coxswain and I put our noses in a cookbook to find a recipe for baking-powder biscuits. *459* had run completely out of bread and there was none to be had ashore. Old French and I thought we knew a great deal about this biscuit business, but we were still a bit nervous. By the time the batter was mixed the whole crew was involved in the big operation, and after the round slices, cut with the cover of the baking-powder tin, had been pushed into the oven, great arguments arose as to the length of time the darn things should cook. After a while the so-called biscuits were carefully taken out. They were flat as pancakes and definitely not a success, but the crews did not condemn them, and every crumb disappeared. I might add, however, that our second attempt was much more satisfactory, with biscuits an inch and a half thick. Eventually, almost everyone had a fling at the culinary arts, although most efforts were usually directed toward camouflaging, not too successfully, the infamous bully beef. Our menu was occasionally varied by trading cigarettes and bully beef with the locals in exchange for eggs, Camembert cheese, and red wine.

While Barney, Chuff-Chuff, and I were taking the usual walk that afternoon, we spotted a familiar character bouncing along in a jeep crossing the bridge over the locks. It was none other than Lieutenant Eric Fisher, the Official Army War Artist, and we greeted each other warmly. He was not free at the time to accept my invitation aboard, but he promised to come down later for supper. God only knew what he would get to eat!

At the appointed hour Barney, Chuff-Chuff, myself, and other officers awaited our guest's appearance in the wardroom, and at dusk Eric and his driver arrived. The crews had cooked up a remarkably good meal, and they looked after the driver while Eric indulged in a small noggin of *vin rouge* and told us with enthusiasm the story of Caen. He had been working furiously, sketching the cream of the subjects, but was finding it difficult to choose the incidents which would make the best paintings. During the course of the evening old John asked Eric how he like our wardroom with its bright red curtains. Eric replied carefully, "It's a bit gay."

"Bit gay?" Shand snorted. "Looks like a woman's boudoir."

As a matter of fact, I agreed with Shand. From some red canvas which we had salvaged from a broken raft on the merchant ship at Gooseberry, John and I had decided to make coverings for the key boards and bookcases; and as curtain material it made a cheering though somewhat effeminate change from the ugly black hangings to which we had been accustomed. The remainder of the evening was spent most pleasantly over a bottle of red wine, and before he departed Eric very kindly gave me a German tin hat as a token of remembrance. After many goodbyes and thank yous, he and his driver drove away and all the ship's company turned in.

On the 21st the winds showed no signs of letting up, and the morning was spent in the usual manner, cleaning ship and guns until all was spick and span. That afternoon Footsie and Joe Bampton, looking very sheepish, were returned to us by an Army major in a jeep. Illegal though it was, they had been in the vicinity of Caen and, from a respectable distance, had taken a good look at the raging battle. They were loaded with souvenirs, including empty cases from shells which had just been fired at the enemy. Both of the lawbreakers nattered on enthusiastically about their thrilling day. As far as I was concerned, it was too dangerous and war-like a manner in which to spend an afternoon.

While Footsie and Joe were out touring, the other crewmen had met a charming old Frenchman, who gave us all a standing invitation to come and drink wine in his vineyard. He and his wife had apparently had a severe time during the German occupation, and this invitation was their way of showing appreciation to their liberators. As the dear old gentleman pointed out, the nicest part of it was that the vineyard was surrounded by a high stone wall, and its occupants would thus be out of sight of the ubiquitous MPs!

On the 22nd of June the wind dropped, puffy cumulous clouds filled the sky, and long gentle swells of the calmed sea sent fingers of water to paw the wreckage littering the sandy beaches. Hundreds of smashed landing craft and LSTs lay broadside at the high water mark, and as I looked at them I wondered how they could ever be refloated. To my astonishment, the salvage officer informed me that the beaches would be clear within a week. Even as we spoke the beach was buzzing with activity, and great bulldozers were pushing sand around and cleaning up the shambles. As it was nearing high tide and the tide gates would soon be opened, I returned to *459,* in time to receive the signal that our three boats of the 29th were to sail back to Portsmouth.

Soon the engines were warmed through and the officers and men were bundled into their most waterproof gear; it would be rough bucking our way

(PAC PA 144582)

home. As the tide gates opened slowly the many landing craft moved off. *459, 465,* and *466,* with all fenders out on the port and starboard sides, squeezed gently through the gate, and the going grew easier. The boats floated down the narrow channel, passed the ugly obstructions at the entrance, and travelled on into the wide open spaces toward *Scylla.* The swells were huge, but the MTBs rode over them like ducks and in no time were passing by the mother-ship. The eagle-eyed Lovelock quickly deciphered a message from her: "We think you will find the weather not too bad. The wind is dropping and the conditions are improving. Good luck." After this information had been received we were off for home, pleased that the weatherman had for once been right. Nevertheless, despite the sunny skies, the spray was heavy, and soon water was leaking down my neck and into my boots. It was the first "bath" I had had for days. It was a long slog home, and when old Nab Tower hove into view it was a welcome sight. The boats were soon in harbour, and after the usual refuelling we went on to *Vernon.* Finally home again, we all relaxed in a steaming hot bath before settling down for a snooze. A great deal of repair work had to be done on the three boats, especially on the rubbing strakes, and the crews were able to relax for the rest of the day, reading letters from home and opening food parcels, which were a real treat after four days of compo-rations.

Daddy Bones spent the night of 23-24 June patrolling "Area Tunny South" in the Assault Area with *461, 462,* and *464.* It was a tinsel night; German aircraft were intermittently dropping the stuff throughout the area, preventing effective use of radar, and this caused much worry to the patrol ship. Not only that, but Daddy Bones with his three companion boats were without a mother-ship. Poor old *Scylla* had been mined during the night, and a destroyer had taken over duties as control ship. No longer did the MTBs have a mother to run to for food and maintenance. *Scylla* would be sorely missed.

The MTBs were vectored four miles west of Le Havre, but when they reached the position only to find a frolicking MacGoffoney, they turned to go back to their original station. On the way Daddy Bones sighted three E-Boats at 300 yards, travelling on an easterly course at a speed of about 30 knots. The 29th's three boats immediately opened fire, aiming at the third E-Boat in line, and closed to 25 yards. In a moment a fierce battle was in progress. The enemy boat crossed Bones's bow, almost causing a collision, and a vigorous chase developed. The E-Boats quickly outdistanced Daddy Bones, although the third of them received severe punishment at point-blank range. Unfortunately, Bones's boat also suffered damage, and two of *461's* crew were seriously wounded. Scobie did his best rendering first aid and making the two lads as comfortable as possible. With the coming of morning, the three MTBs returned to the Assault Area to land their casualties and then proceeded back across the Channel to Portsmouth.

Saturday was *462's* day for inspection, and Bobby Moyse, looking very serious, was on tour that morning accompanied by Jessman, his Number One, who wore a big smile. Looking over one of the guns, Bobby detected a small spot which was not oiled, and inquired, "Who looks after this gun?"

"It's either Able Seaman Parks No. 1 or Parks No. 2." The Parks twins were identical in appearance, which made things difficult for the commanding officer.

"Well, summon one of them," ordered Bobby in a severe Senior Officer's tone. Jessman yelled down the hatch for one of the Parks, and in short order an alert-looking young seaman appeared and saluted the CO smartly. "Are you the one who looks after this gun?" Bobby asked.

"No, Sir, it's Parks No. 2."

Parks No. 2 was then summoned, and was soon standing beside his brother. Bobby, still inspecting the gun, looked up to be confronted by the two Parks. Thoroughly confused, he asked, "Which of you is Parks No. 2?"

"I am, Sir."

"You're sure you're Parks No. 2?"

"Yes, Sir."

"Right," replied the bewildered Bobby. "Oil up this part of the gun."

The interrupted inspection continued with pomp and ceremony, but in a short while the CO had stopped again. "Who looks after this gun?"

The First Lieutenant replied, "Parks No. 1, Sir."

Again the two lads were summoned; they came on the double and listened attentively while their visibly shaken CO repeated the same procedure step by step. The whole performance jarred poor old Bobby to such an extent that late into the afternoon he could still be heard mumbling to himself, "Parks No. 1 and Parks No. 2."

In *463* Motor Mechanic Monroe was hard at work cleaning up his engine room. While walking down the cats that lovely Saturday morning I caught sight of him as he poked his head out the hatch for a breath of fresh air. "How are things going, Tubby?" I enquired.

"Fine, Sir, except I'm getting too thin for my clothes," he replied with a grin.

I went on, laughing, but old Monroe really did look thinner. I'm sure he had lost 20 pounds since joining the MTBs.

In the meantime, Dave Killam's boat, *460,* was undergoing a 48-hour refit at BP in Hythe, and Dave and Howie were on leave. MTBs were damaging their propellers faster than they could be repaired, for the Assault Area was filled

Opposite: The ill-fated MTB 460. (PAC PA144582)

with the wreckage of many mined ships as well as with timbers from the Cherbourg docks, which the Germans had blown up just before the Americans broke through into the port. These water-logged obstacles floated around in the Channel and caused hundreds of craft to be slipped and reslipped for repairs to or replacement of their rudders and propellers.

On 1 July, *459, 460,* and *465* were on their way across to Normandy. There was a bit of a swell, but the boats still managed to make 20 knots, with Footsie and I keeping a sharp lookout for floating debris. Some of the floating timbers were almost as large as telephone poles, and we had to make drastic alterations in course to avoid them. We had travelled about 20 miles when suddenly there was a terrific thud, followed by vibrations so violent that *459* was nearly shaken to pieces. I immediately signalled the boats astern to stop. Poor old *459* had struck a submerged timber, damaging two of her propellers. She slowed to a stop and the three other boats came up alongside. It was the first time *459* had failed her master. I realized that in her injured condition she would have to return to Portsmouth, so I called across to Dave Killam to act as Senior Officer, and he and Chuff-Chuff carried on in the direction of Normandy. Then *459* turned to limp back to harbour on two engines; the vibrations were teeth-rattling, but she managed to do a steady ten knots. On

arrival I contacted the engineer officer, who informed me that BP could slip us, but that unfortunately the job could not be done until the next day.

At about 1700 the next day we got back to Portsmouth with two new propellers, and as soon as I arrived the Coastal Force officer in charge of *Vernon* told me that Captain McLaughlin, Captain Coastal Force, wished me to ring him up immediately. I dashed to the phone to put in the call and in a few moments the Captain's subdued voice came over the wire. "Hello, Law, I have some very bad news for you. We have just received a signal from the Assault Area. MTB *460* struck a mine this morning and was blown up. There are only six survivors. Both officers as well as nine ratings are missing and two bodies have been picked up. We cannot tell you how sorry we are about this terrible disaster. My staff and I offer our sincere sympathy to you and your flotilla."

Dazed by the sudden loss, I mumbled my thanks, and Captain McLaughlin bade me goodnight. The horrible waste of war was brought home to all the officers and crews of the 29th when they learned the sad news. The next morning there were no smiles. The crews and officers went quietly about their work, outwardly calm, yet inside throbbed a terrible pain, caused not only by the loss of their comrades, but also by thoughts of others to whom those comrades were near and dear.

Later in the morning, Chuff-Chuff arrived in *465*. We had left the bodies of Able Seaman C. Ashmore and G. Grant at Haslar Pier to be taken to the morgue at the hospital. Chuff-Chuff was pale and somber. He had not yet recovered from the shock of seeing his friend, Dave Killam, blown up in front of him as they returned from patrol on the morning of 2 July. In the Flotilla Office he told me the tragic story, his voice low. He had carried out a thorough search of the area in which the disaster had occurred, and had succeeded in picking up the six survivors and two bodies. After a long search another MTB flotilla had come to relieve them and to carry on the search.

That afternoon at 1400, MTBs *459, 464,* and *462* sailed out the gates of the Eastern Solent, passed Nab Tower, and sped swiftly down the swept channel to Normandy. Our thoughts were far away, and there were few words spoken. On entering the Assault Area we closed our control ship, a frigate, originally an American destroyer escort but now part of the Royal Navy. It possessed good speed, a magnificent radar set, and numerous rapid-firing guns.

The frigate warned us of the terrible mines, believed to be pressure mines, which had already accounted for the sinking of a considerable number of ships, and then we were given our assignment for the night. Our unit was to proceed to a rendezvous position eight miles off Cap d'Antifer. The frigate went on ahead of us, travelling at only three knots because of the mines. We MTBs had been instructed to speed as rapidly as possible over the mined area, the theory being that we should then have a better chance of survival. Uneasily, we sailed out into the swept channel on a northward course, which was later altered eastward toward Cap d'Antifer and the frigate. It was nerve-wracking to pass through the wreckage littering the mysterious, oily seas, for in the dim twilight every object took on the appearance of a destructive mine. The little boats were continually swinging hard to port or hard to starboard to avoid the sinister black shapes, only to identify these a moment later as innocent wooden boxes.

We sped on through the greasy waters and before long joined our control ship, the frigate. Throughout that long night we were tormented by the shore batteries. Our tension was intensified by the apparent attraction of the mined area for our boats, and we constantly had to steer away from the area. When the patrol was over we returned, exhausted, to the Assault Area, deciding to spend the day tied up to the famous "Mulberry" artificial harbour. After snatching a few hours of sleep, some of us went ashore. John Shand, Bish, Bobby, and I tramped slowly down the pontoon bridge which joined the floating pier to the shore of Arromanches, and when we finally reached the end of it a soldier stopped us, demanding our shore passes. None of us had one, and when we asked him where they could be obtained, he said that the NOIC at Arromanches might issue them, with emphasis on the "might". We walked on into the little French town and soon located the NOIC's home, again a beautiful villa enhanced by a tree-flanked boulevard. Trust the good old Navy to pick the best spots! The other officers waited outside while I went in to humbly request the passes. The NOIC's reply was abrupt and firm—NO. As at Port aux Courseulles, we were limited to swimming and walking up and down the once-glorious beach, now covered with the remnants of broken ships and oddments of destroyed equipment. Disgusted with the endless red tape and restrictions, I decided I would do my best to forget about the war for just this one afternoon. On a nice grassy plateau beneath a German radar set, overlooking the Mulberry, I fell fast asleep in the hot sunshine.

At the end of the day *459, 464,* and *462,* found themselves embarked on a new adventure. We left our frigate six miles west of Cap d'Antifer and crept slowly toward the cliffs between Cap d'Antifer and Cap de la Hève, thus placing ourselves in an enviable strategic position. It was not quite dark as we moved gently along, the moon had made its appearance to the south of us, and the high shoreline loomed even larger as the boats grew closer to the towering skyline. It had been customary for the E- and R-Boats to hide under these cliffs, while the enemy convoys they protected slipped through to Le Havre.

Don Bradford's flotilla was about eight miles south of us off Cap de la Hève, the moon had risen, and everything was in our favour. From our position under the cliffs we could see anything that might poke its nose around Cap de la Hève, and anything on its way from Fécamp to Cap de la Hève would have to pass close by. Our courageous frigate lay only eight miles off the enemy coast.

Raising my binoculars, I began carefully searching the horizon in the direction of Le Havre, and I suddenly spotted a black speck moving round the Cape. It was followed by another, and then another, and soon there were nine little dots coming toward us. Three against nine. It would be quite a battle.

Simpson, the radar operator, soon picked up echoes at 2,000 yards dead ahead, and Footsie signalled the frigate that we had picked up the enemy. Sure enough, nine E-Boats, hugging the coast, were moving toward our position, and I grimly imagined their surprise when they found the opposition so well established in their hideaway. *459* moved off, steadily increasing speed, followed closely astern by Bobby and Bish. The enemy were now 1,500 yards from us, and both sides were closing dead ahead. It was exactly at midnight when our three boats opened fire at 1,400 yards, and at 1,200 yards all guns were blazing away at the leading E-Boat. We then switched targets to the third E-Boat in line, and under our concentrated volley it burst into flames and was left in a sinking condition. His comrades quickly made smoke, obscuring our view, but we could still see the glow of the fire through the haze, and I very much doubt if the craft could have made Le Havre.

The E-Boats were on the run, and they were running straight into Don Bradford's unit. A battle developed between Don and the scampering E-Boats, which altered course again and came back toward us. The friendly moon silhouetted them clearly against the horizon, and at the same time made it difficult for the E-Boats to see us against the background of the cliffs. We let them come to within a thousand yards before firing. Our tracer streamed over them, and the 29th closed to 400 yards. The E-Boats, though now only eight, were still numerically superior, and we received a quantity of flak in return. Unfortunately, after doing a good bit of damage to these gentlemen, *459* was forced to disengage when a shell hit her in the W/T (wireless transmitter) cabin, leaving a gaping hole where the cabin had been and narrowly missing poor old McAulley. We had also been hit up forward by an incendiary and a fire had started. As the unit disengaged, Simpson yelled up to the bridge, "An aircraft is dive-bombing us, Sir!" A *Heinkel* screamed over us, and Able Seaman Dublack, the Oerlikon gunner, immediately opened fire. The other two boats joined in. A bomb crashed just astern of *459*, sending up a huge column of water and shaking the living daylights out of the three MTBs. As soon as that incident was over the shore batteries started up, and we disengaged behind a smokescreen, drastically altering course so the enemy would not be able to get our range.

In the meantime, another unit of E-Boats had come down from Fécamp and run straight into the E-Boats from which we had just disengaged. A terrific

Opposite: Dawn from 459's bridge. (PAC PA143048)

all-German battle ensued, and the air was filled with massive quantities of green and yellow tracer zipping back and forth. The E-Boats were having it out between themselves. They finally got themselves sorted out, and the firing ceased. By this time *459* had squelched the forward fire, and having pretty well licked her wounds she went in for another run at the *Schnellboote,* presenting them with a brief, hot, visiting card. Not anxious to continue our acquaintanceship, they ran for Le Havre, only to be greeted by Don Bradford's flotilla. On the way out Bobby's starboard engine broke down and he was ordered to rejoin the control ship. As *462* limped away to the frigate another dirty *Heinkel* dive-bombed her, leaving Bobby rather weak in the knees.

At 0115 Bish and I sighted two German 'M' class minesweepers on the horizon, making their way toward us escorted by two R-Boats. Bish and I started to shadow them, plotting their course and speed, and when satisfied with the estimate we turned in toward the small convoy for a torpedo attack. But we were sighted, and the enemy opened up with flocks of starshells plus 88-mm shells, which came crashing angrily about our tiny vessels. The German shore batteries just couldn't be excluded from the excitement and they added a most uncomfortable barrage. Nevertheless, we replied so effectively with our guns that the convoy turned back toward Le Havre and Don Bradford carried on the pursuit.

Dawn came at last, soothing our jangled nerves. There is something about the dawn. Perhaps just the fact that it is no longer dark gives one a feeling of security, a feeling that the danger is over, or can at least be guarded against.

That welcome daylight, dissolving the horrible nightmare, was like a gift coming direct from the Almighty. We looked forward to it with anxious anticipation after a night of action. It seemed to bring back reality, and to place a value on the world around us. The crews of *459* and *464* were absolutely exhausted, both physically and mentally, and the three wounded boats limped back to Portsmouth for repairs.

The following afternoon in Haslar Cemetery the crews and officers of the 29th Flotilla paid their final tributes to Able Seamen George Grant and George Ashmore. The beautiful, simple service was held in a typical, old English chapel. Outside the lovely trees stood like peaceful, sympathetic statues, while inside our prayers and thoughts went out to our two comrades, and to the others who were still missing: Lieutenant Dave Killam, DSC; Lieutenant Howard Hunt; Petty Officer Motor Mechanic George; Telegraphist Peter Thompson; Stoker Mechanics L. Lawson, E.A. Button, and J. Hartley; and Telegraphist A.W. Rowe, an English lad who had been on loan to us. The *Last Post* was sounded, and as we listened with heads bowed in respect, our hearts were heavy. When the final note fell on the still air, we knew that two of our comrades were at peace.

On 7 July, Glen Creba in MTB *463* and Barney Marshall in *466* carried out the usual patrol in the Assault Area, guarding the anchorage. This time they were confronted with a new problem, the human torpedo. Actually this was made up of two torpedoes: the male torpedo carried one person, who sat forward in a glass-enclosed dome, and attached to the male was the female, or live torpedo. The "crew" of this type of weapon was usually a youngster between fourteen and eighteen years of age, chosen for his small size. The female was manually released by the lad in the male torpedo. The first night on which this invention was used, six or seven ships were sunk, so on the night of 7 July, Glen and Barney were keeping a sharp lookout for the glass-domed troublemakers, planning to finish off any that they saw with small depth charges. Our MTBs now carried only six of these, as we had been refitted with torpedoes. It was a ghastly night for Glen and Barney, for no matter where they sailed, mines were set off. They must have set off at least 25 mines that night, and the officers and crews, their nerves raw, were feeling the strain.

At 0500 on 8 July, *463* and *466* were searching for human torpedoes along the eastern edge of Area Sword. They were travelling at 15 knots when suddenly Creba's boat set off a submerged mine. A gigantic column of water gushed high in the air, completely immersing *463* and almost causing her to disappear from sight. After emerging from the geyser of water she started to settle quickly by the stern, but, strangely enough, casualties were light, chiefly consisting of sprained legs and arms and some bad bruises. Barney rushed alongside in *466* and quickly took on all Glen's crew. Poor Cunningham, who

Two of the 29th MTBs with 466 outboard. Note that 466 has been refitted with torpedo tubes, while the inboard boat still has the racks of small depth charges. The white star on the forecastle was to indicate to aircraft that this was an Allied boat. (PAC PA144573)

had just joined the flotilla as a spare officer and was on his first trip in an MTB, was swimming around in the chilly water wondering what had happened in the past few seconds. Glen Creba and Dick Paddon stayed on board *463,* endeavouring to salvage the craft by lightening ship in hope that she would float. She was taken in tow, and two 'C' class MGBs came into the area to lend a hand. Everything possible was done to lighten *463,* but all efforts were in vain, and eventually "Abandon Ship" was ordered by the disheartened CO. The last they saw of her was a triangle of her bow surrounded by bubbles just before she slipped rapidly under the surface at 0700. Two tears welled in the Captain's eyes when only wreckage was left on the surface, and the officers and crew turned their heads sadly away from the sea which had claimed their home. Another tragic chapter had been added to the history of the flotilla.

Glen and his crew were returned to the Assault Area and put on board a Polish destroyer, where they received warm food and care for the wounded. They were then taken to Portsmouth and given seven days' leave. A new boat was waiting upon their return—MTB *485.* This boat was fitted with new 1,500-horsepower engines, which gave it a speed of 42 knots, far superior to the other boats.

Our whole routine was thrown out of kilter by the loss of *460* and *463,* and to make up a team for operations in the British Assault Area, *459* joined Daddy Bones in *461* and Bish in *464.* On the night of 8-9 July we were in the Assault Area, accompanied by Lieutenant-Commander Freddie Dunlop, DSC, RN, the signal officer on CCF's staff, who rode in my boat. We were lying between Le Havre and D'Antifer, about three miles from the cliffs, while two English Short MGBs patrolled seven miles northward. The boats were silent, the sea calm, and the air still, until suddenly a violent action broke out north of us. The engines of our three boats started up, the crews hastened to action stations, and we moved off in the direction of the battle. The RT was buzzing with excited chatter, and as we steadily increased speed, we saw that one of the two English boats was on fire, the red flames glowing ominously against the sky. The Senior Officer of the gunboats called us up to say that since his craft was damaged in the bows and taking in water, he was disengaging. He requested that we come in and pick up the survivors of *434,* the boat that was ablaze. By this time Daddy Bones, Bish, and I were travelling at maximum speed, but we couldn't get near the MGB because the enemy had it surrounded. We decided to attack, and roared in at high speed in battle formation, spraying the ten R-Boats with our fire. The enemy craft were heavily armed with 37-mm guns, and a hot and intense action was soon under way. We got in some nice hits, but at the same time were subjected to a fierce barrage of yellow and green tracer.

I particularly admired our guest Freddie Dunlop, the signal officer, during the action. Many months in the past he had broken his back, but in spite of the great agony the injury still caused him he continued to climb up and down the narrow ladder to the W/T cabinet, and efficiently attended to the defects in the RT, which had become temperamental at the critical moment. While he was below in the radar cabin a German 37-mm shell struck *459* on the starboard side, exploded in the coxswain's cabin, and put the radar out of action. Freddie fell to the deck in the nick of time, and a spray of shell-splinters flew over him. Peculiarly enough, Simpson wasn't even scratched, but the radar cabin was a mess. After the shell exploded, Freddie didn't move for several long moments, during which I feared the worst, but much to my relief he pulled himself cautiously to his feet a minute later. *464* had her ensign shot away, her usual punishment.

The action had become so intense and one-sided that we disengaged and roared away making smoke, although still pursued by the yellow 37-mm shells. When the falling of the shells had subsided, I reduced speed and called up the other two boats to get a report on their casualties. After learning that Daddy Bones had no casualties, although his boat was damaged, I called Bish.

"Hello Tony, Tony, Tony; this is Bish. Have one killed and one wounded and damage to the boat. I've been shot in the ass. Over."

"Tony. Roger. Out."

When John Shand heard Bish's report of his wound, he roared with laughter. It had indeed sounded very funny coming over the air, but the news of another death among our comrades renewed our grim determination to save those on the burning *434*.

We got back into battle formation and went into the attack. The R-Boats had stopped moving and were lying off the British MGB *434*. Another hot engagement took place, and again our three boats were forced to disengage under heavy fire from the enemy, who were aided by the shore batteries. But we were leaving our mark: one of the R-Boats was on fire. I decided that the best course to follow would be to have Daddy Bones make a smokescreen while Bish and I went into the hornet's nest to give battle to the enemy, acting for the third time as a decoy. It was a fierce moment for all three boats. Bones, who was soon between the R-Boats and the burning *434*, made a beautiful half-circle and closed the fired ship. Then Bish and I, sheltered by the curtain of smoke which hung between us and the enemy, nipped back toward the survivors. The R-Boats had ceased firing and lay about 800 yards away while we closed the inferno, which was now tinting the smokescreen with a pinkish glow. Ammunition exploding into the air looked like vast swarms of fireflies. Finally we sighted two Carley floats near us in the water with several pathetic figures clinging to them for dear life. They were all picked up by Daddy Bones and Bish; fortunately, only one of *434's* crew had been killed. The three MTBs, after making sure that all survivors were aboard, quickly left the burning wreck of *434,* now settling fast. We made haste toward the frigate which was escorting the remaining MGB back to the anchorage.

The sun rose sluggishly, giving us a nasty, bleak morning as we sailed into the Assault Area in search of a hospital ship. We were ordered to one frigate only to be refused by her, and from there we were directed to pull up alongside a cruiser and land the unwounded survivors. Dampened by a dreary drizzle, we helped the haggard, blanket-wrapped survivors up the steep side of the cruiser, which was being used as a depot ship. We still had some seriously wounded casualties aboard who were in need of immediate attention. There was one poor English lad, his face ghostly pale, bearing up courageously, but I was afraid he would die before we could get him to a hospital ship. Fortunately, the cruiser was able to direct us to the mercy ship, and after much yawing in and out between anchored vessels, the three Canadian MTBs and the British MGB reached its side. Freddie Dunlop was standing by me on the bridge as I called up to two sick-bay attendants who were propped up against the ship's rail, looking completely bored. "We have some serious casualties and would like to land them."

One of the attendants replied, "Just a minute, Sir," and slowly dragged himself away from the rail to saunter off for the surgeon.

A saucy Army captain appeared in a few moments and shouted down in a shrill, bossy voice, "We're filled up and can't take any more except on the deck. Even then we can't attend to them." Then he nipped down and boarded the boat, and after looking at our casualties he muttered in a very audible tone, "Can't take them. They're too serious." Although what he said was probably true, I felt very badly for the wounded men who lay on the upper deck of *464* listening to these callous remarks. The surgeon continued, "There's an LST anchored three miles from here that can probably take them," and with that he scrambled back aboard the hospital ship. Freddie Dunlop's face was red with rage at the whole performance, and I learned that he later sent a furiously severe signal to the hospital ship.

We had no choice but to start up the engines, and my thoughts suddenly turned to an old friend, the battleship HMS *Rodney,* who I was sure would help us. We steamed toward where she was anchored, looking like the Rock of Gibraltar, and after making fast I asked if we could land our casualties. A smart young marine told us to wait a moment, and nipped away to return with a dear old Surgeon Commander, who said he would be able to take all our casualties and assured me they would receive the best of care.

Opposite: Aerial photo of HMS Rodney, *friend of the 29th MTB Flotilla and the "good Samaritan" who lent aid in time of need. (PAC PMR77-290)*

After the casualties had been landed we were faced with the problem of persuading Bish to follow them aboard. He wanted to take his boat back to Portsmouth, even though he couldn't sit down! The Surgeon Commander finally told him that if he didn't get his wound attended to immediately, he was likely to be in the hospital for weeks. That did it, and Joe Adams became Commanding Officer of *464*. We thanked *Rodney* for everything and the four boats started their slow journey back.

The British MGB's engines were defective, and the weather was foul. Water lapped through the large hole in *459's* starboard side, despite our having stuffed it with all kinds of sweaters and other wearing apparel. When we arrived at *Vernon,* worn and weary, everything was soaking wet and my hands were so cold I could hardly move them.

Back at the anchorage, Bish and the others aboard *Rodney* were being pampered by their hosts. Bish had even been given the Captain's day cabin, which was suggestive of the royal suite in a luxury hotel. At one point the Captain's steward knocked on the door of the cabin where Bish was lying in state and said, "Excuse me, Sir, but we've got to fire another two shells–the

last of our ammunition. I'm afraid you'll be disturbed, and we're awfully sorry.'' After the shells had been fired, two tugs commenced to tow *Rodney* out of the Normandy anchorage as a precaution against mines. No one dared breathe until she was in deep water, except Bish, who was sound asleep and oblivious of such mundane matters. At 1600 that afternoon, somewhere between Normandy and Portsmouth, Bish had the chunk of shrapnel removed from his sit-upon, after which he snuggled deeper into the lap of luxury and wondered how much leave he would get. The other wounded had all been attended to and everyone was doing well.

Next morning, 10 July, I was sitting in the Flotilla Office when a signal arrived: "To the Senior Officer, 29th Flotilla, from HMS *Rodney.* Request car be sent to Stokes Bay Pier for Lieutenant Bishop, RCNVR.''

Some time later Bish arrived in a magnificent car, driven by, to quote the English, a smashing little Wren. Bish grinned exuberantly and chortled, ''Boy, was I treated like a king! Only the best . . . even the Captain's day cabin!'' I sent a signal to *Rodney* expressing our appreciation for all she had done for us.

On the night of 13-14 July, Daddy Bones in *461* was Senior Officer, accompanied by Bobby in *462* and Chuff-Chuff in *465.* Both Daddy Bones and Chuff-Chuff had had their boats fitted with torpedo tubes, but those for Bobby's boat were still sitting on the pier at *Vernon.* Everything was quiet in the Assault Area. The control ship was 12 miles off Le Havre patrolling in a line parallel to the shore, while Bones and his clan sat four to five miles off the same port. The shore batteries were behaving themselves, leaving the boats in peace. All at once the stillness was broken by the control ship, vectoring Bones in the direction of Le Havre. A small convoy had been picked up, and as soon as *461's* radar had contacted it the three boats started to shadow the convoy to plot its course and speed. Bones could see two 'M' class minesweepers escorted by eight E- or R-Boats, and Scobie and Robertson were hard at work on the plotting. The enemy had not seen them and everything was going according to plan. Torpedoes were brought to the ready, and Bobby was ordered to detach himself and act as decoy. *461* and *465* were well ahead of the enemy, running on a parallel course—a nice position for a torpedo attack. At 1,000 yards they turned in toward the convoy and closed. The range shortened swiftly . . . 900 yards . . . 800 . . . 700 . . . 600 . . . "Ready both'' . . . ''Fire'' . . . and the torpedoes were gone. But at the crucial moment the enemy altered course and sighted the three boats. Bobby bravely took on the two 'M' class minesweepers together with eight escorts, but his efforts were in vain. All three boats had been spotted and a fierce battle began, with the enemy's efforts ably abetted by the Le Havre shore batteries. In the face of such odds, the MTBs, after a spirited encounter, were forced to disengage behind a comfortable smokescreen.

A serious casualty had been suffered by *462,* the unfortunate lad being one of the Parks twins. His injuries were so severe, it seemed very doubtful if even the best surgical brains could save the wounded lad. The two brothers had gone through the Navy together, but now it would be a long time, if ever, before there would again be a Parks No. 1 and a Parks No. 2.

After catching their collective breath the three MTBs closed the control ship, where they learned that one of the echoes on her radar scan had vanished immediately after the MTBs' torpedoes had been fired. It looked as if they had scored a hit. When dawn broke the boats sailed back to the anchorage and landed Parks, whose condition had become even more critical. Then *461, 462,* and *465* returned to Portsmouth.

It was 14 July, and *459, 464,* and *466* were on patrol about 12 miles off Le Havre. Our control ship was a frigate, HMS *Duff,* commanded by Lieutenant-Commander Freddie Brock, DSC, RCNVR, who had become a very good friend of the flotilla and had helped us with emergency repairs. On this lovely, calm night the sky was slightly clouded, but visibility was good for five miles, and the three boats rocked gently over the smooth swell. At 2354 the silence was broken by *Duff,* who vectored our unit north at 20 knots. We skimmed swiftly over the black, oily waters, and it wasn't long before Simpson picked up three echoes dead ahead at 1,500 yards. Our three craft went into battle formation, Order 7. *459, 464,* and *466* surprised the enemy, which appeared to be three E-Boats laying mines, and the battle started at close range. *459* moved in between the second and third E-Boats and fired at 20 yards—point-blank range. A rain of tracer flashed back and forth, and the intensity of the battle was terrific. As the firing increased in accuracy, a 20-mm shell hit *459's* pom-pom loading tray, putting it completely out of action, but, luckily, the ammunition in the tray did not explode. Our three boats altered to port toward Le Havre to give chase to the enemy, who were racing away at full speed. We chased the *Schnellboote* to within a mile of the breakwater at Le Havre where the enemy made smoke, although they had already outdistanced us and were entering the harbour. Toward the end of the action our gun-fire was ineffective because the range was too great, and *459* seemed to be suffering from some strange ailment. She was extremely sluggish and could not maintain a good speed; her boost was high and the revs were low. The engagement was broken off, and our unit turned 180° and made for the control ship. As we altered course I realized the outer breakwater of Le Havre was uncomfortably close, and, fully expecting the shore batteries to give us a hearty reception at any moment, I decided that we should make smoke to cloud up that good visibility. But my fears were soon laid to rest, for the shore guns appeared to be asleep and didn't even put a starshell over our heads.

Pushing mines away from 459 in Normandy waters. (PAC C127023)

With that problem solved, I turned my attention back to *459*, who seemed to be low in the bow and wasn't planing properly. I sent Shand below to investigate, and he was up again in short order to report that she had been hit by a 20-mm shell below the waterline and that the forward bulkhead was flooded. I immediately informed *Duff* of our mishap and she instructed us to close her. With much chuffing we finally manoeuvred alongside, and she soon had the situation well in hand. The water was removed with an electric pump, and a chippie slapped a tingle over *459's* wound. Nothing could be done for the pom-pom, so it was out of action for the rest of the night. Freddie Brock told me that they had intercepted a message from the three E-Boats, which said that one of them had suffered 11 casualties. It looked as if we had roughed up one of the *Schnellboote* pretty badly.

After drinking a nice quiet cup of cocoa on Freddie's bridge, I thanked him for his assistance and returned to weary *459*. Our three small boats proceeded back out to the patrol position, where we remained until morning. When our nightly stint had been concluded we left our posts and passed into the anchorage. Our drooping eyes were abruptly opened when we suddenly set off a mine, which sent tons of water flying hundreds of feet into the air. Cautioned by the incident, *459* reduced speed and crept down the swept channel to Mulberry, where she made fast alongside the repair ship to have the pom-pom tray welded. Once this had been attended to, we breakfasted and then fell into our bunks to catch some badly needed sleep. Tired groans and sighs soon dissolved into the deep, peaceful breathing of heavy sleep. The weary were at rest.

The officers and crews of the MTBs were beginning to show the strain caused by the months of nerve-wracking patrols. The stress and irregular meals were responsible for many of us losing weight. The 29th was battle-weary, and we were beginning to feel that we could not last much longer under the severe conditions—mine threats, pounding shore batteries, and vicious dive bombers roaring out of the night and putting the fear of God into us. Off Seine Bay the nights had been sheer terror, with hot fierce engagements at close range with the enemy. The personnel of the 29th were falling victims to horrible, haunting fears, and the boats, whose arduous task of defending the anchorage had almost burnt them out, were badly in need of repair.

On 15-16 July we were once again on the job off Le Havre, again with a feeling that some unusual, unpredictable thing was about to happen. The flotilla, consisting of *459*, *464*, and *466*, was having a great deal of trouble getting into its assigned position about three miles off Cap de la Héve. At 2337 we were shelled by the Trouville shore batteries, which were situated on the

459 taken in tow after being hit by shore batteries, 15/16 July 1944. (PAC C127034)

south shore of Seine Bay, and the enemy shells fell uncomfortably close. *Duff* vectored us onto a radar contact, but it turned out to be just another ironized MacGoffoney, and once again we were heavily shelled by the shore batteries. Finally, in desperation, we zig-zagged out of range behind a cloud of our chemical smoke. At midnight *Duff* picked up another radar echo indicating a small convoy coming from Le Havre, and sticking close to the shoreline as it travelled toward D'Antifer. As our boats moved into position for a torpedo attack, three miles off Cap de la Héve, German aircraft started dropping flares overhead. Expecting to be dive-bombed, we stopped dead so that our wakes would not give away our position. Then Simpson yelled up the voicepipe, "Shore batteries Green 90 have opened up." Starting up again, our three MTBs began zig-zagging once more.

A salvo of shells crashed around us, sending sheets of water into the air. A second salvo was right on its heels, and this time a shell hit *459* in the engine room with a loud and devastating explosion. The coxswain and I were pinned down in the bridge by a piece of the engine room deck, and *459* began settling rapidly by the stern. After the first panic-stricken moment, French, enraged by the piece of debris and stimulated by fear, was able to free us both. I quickly grabbed the RT, directing Barney to come alongside and Joe Adams to carry out a full-speed smokescreen between us and the enemy shore. Barney also made a smokescreen, which covered us completely. Rescue parties were already trying to get into the engine room, but with two feet of water covering the hatch, all their attempts failed. From stern to amidships, *459* was completely under water, her bow thrust into the air at a 45° angle. Carley floats were thrown over the side and all crewmen were mustered. P/O Motor Mechanic E. Dawson and Stoker Motor Mechanic M.J. McMahon were missing, and the other Stoker Motor Mechanic had been wounded in his face and arms by tiny pieces of shrapnel and was suffering from shock. Barney had to wait until the smoke had cleared before he could come alongside, and I was afraid that *459* would slip under the water before he could get to us. Lovelock came running up to the bridge asking permission to throw one of the lead-covered Confidential Books over the side. Armed with my OK, he disappeared down the hatch, returning a moment later with the CB chest. Just as he was about to throw it over a horrible thought occurred to me and I yelled, "Stop! Don't throw that thing overboard unless you have to, or I'll be writing reports about the damned things for the rest of my life."

MTB *464* finally managed to come alongside to rescue *459's* crew. The enemy, curious to know what was going on behind Joe Adam's glorious smokescreen, was still firing starshells overhead. Once we were all on board, *464* ran back and forth, keeping the smokescreen intact, while *459* was taken under tow by *466*. It was impossible to get at the bodies below because the whole stern was submerged, and we had no diving apparatus with which to enter the flooded morgue that had once been our engine room. The tide was with us, but *466,* burdened as she was, could only make four knots, and we had six miles to go before we could close HMS *Duff.*

There was an amusing character on board *466,* Ernie Byfield, an American correspondent. A rather spherical, elderly gentleman, he found it difficult to climb through the hatches, and whenever he got stuck the crews had to assist in unsticking him. I admired Ernie; he had a 26-year-old son in the American Navy, which meant that he himself was no spring chicken, and he certainly did not have to expose himself out in these funny little boats. After the severe night Ernie felt badly in need of a drink to steady his nerves (purely medicinal purposes, please note), and I know I could have done with one, or perhaps two, after the tragic loss of our comrades and dear old *459.* How she floated with her bow straight up in the air, I don't know; she was like a bobbing bottle half full of water. In *466* Barney was doing a fine job, but it was slow going, and he had to steer hard to port to keep a steady course. Eventually, *464* stopped making smoke, and as the boats were now well away from the gruesome Cap de la Héve, we all felt more at ease.

Two 'C' class MGBs had been vectored by the control frigate to escort us, and after many hours we came alongside the black silhouette of *Duff.* At first the electric pumps were put to work to pump the water out of *459,* but this task was soon abandoned as futile, for the hole in her side was 14 feet long and the full height of the hull. Then I went aboard *459* with a steel cable which I was going to try to shackle to the towing pennant, so as to lift her stern out of the water. Yet, since I was up to my waist in water while standing on the Oerlikon gun bandstand, this plan was also given up. Nothing else could be done, so *459* was secured alongside *Duff* and my crew and I climbed aboard.

The Chief Engineer very kindly loaned me his cabin, gave me a pair of pyjamas, and took my wet clothes down to the engine room to dry. Next morning they were returned to me, warm and dry, but somewhat stiff. As soon as I had dressed, I walked back to the stern of HMS *Duff,* where *459,* looking very submissive and pathetic, was tagging along in tow. *Duff* was steaming cautiously down the swept channel, but she eventually anchored to wait out the rest of the day. Salvage operations on *459* commenced immediately. She was first dragged around forward of *Duff,* then a wire cable leading to the anchor winch was placed around her stern, and she was hauled out of the water. The fumes of the hundred-octane gas threatened to bowl us over. After the bodies of poor Dawson and dear old McMahon had been taken out, we discovered that there was nothing left of the engine which had been the target of the 88-mm shell, and that fragments of both engines were scattered all over the engine room. I found an apparently intact, unopened case of Haig and Haig and gave it to Barney for safe-keeping, as looting had become prevalent. The next course of action was to strip *459* of all valuable fittings and transfer them to *464* and *466*, for in the Assault Area spare parts were snapped as quickly as possible by anyone who could get his hands on them. After these matters had been attended to, a salvage ship came alongside and scooped up my poor old boat. My heart lay heavily in my chest as I watched the salvage ship move off toward the beach with *459* dangling from one arm of her derrick and a British MTB from the other. Oddly enough, the British craft had been in a collision the night before with MTB *629*, which had been my boat until 1943.

That afternoon we received orders to bury our dead at sea, and we were grateful for the presence of Father Moreau, who had consoled us throughout the last two shattering days.* The burial took place near the Trinity light vessel, *Juno*, in the outer area of the anchorage. *464* and *466* tied up alongside each other, and on their decks gathered their crewmen and those of *459*. The sun shone brilliantly, the sea lay calm, and a simple mourning service was held on the upper decks of the two MTBs. Dawson's and McMahon's comrades, quiet and sorrowful, stood motionless, scarcely able to believe that they had lost their two friends. Both had been fine men, possessing many sterling qualities, and as we bent our heads in prayer we hoped that their sacrifice had not been in vain. At the same time we were also burying an English rating who had been killed in the British MTB, and Father Moreau said prayers for all three of the unfortunate lads. He then spoke a few words to the assembled company, and his remarks were especially comforting to the men of *459*. The bodies were slid gently over the side, and a 21-round volley was fired for each man, the crack of the rifles shattering the stillness. The service had concluded, and solemn faced officers and crews returned to their posts of duty. Laden with the heavy-hearted survivors, the boats moved slowly toward home.

By this time the 29th had borne the strain of warfare day after day for almost two months. The flotilla had lost three craft, and casualties amounted to 37 per cent of the personnel. The remaining craft, long overdue for refits, were in a shocking condition, and crewmen were fatigued almost to the breaking point. Nevertheless, Daddy Bones, as acting Senior Officer, had returned to the Assault Area with *461*, *462*, *465*, and *466*. Coastal Force Mobile Unit 1 (CFMU No. 1) under the charge of Commander Brind, RN, was now installed at Arromanches near the Mulberry. This unit consisted of 18 trucks and repair ships engaged in maintaining Coastal Force. Daddy Bones's five ships remained in Normandy until 1 August, and during this time only one action took place—

*Reverend Cecil H. Moreau, Chaplain, RCN, had already won an OBE for his previous service with the 29th Flotilla in Normandy.

a torpedo attack on a German convoy off Le Havre. The attack was moderately successful, and the unit was believed to have sunk one of the enemy ships. Barney Marshall was badly wounded in one arm, but his First Lieutenant, Joe Bampton, took over *466* without breaking formation. All in all the action was exceedingly well executed, receiving high commendations afterward.

During the last days in Normandy, rations were very limited, but at one point Daddy Bones came into possession of two food parcels addressed to Corney Burke (Lieutenant Commander C.A. Burke, DSC and two Bars). Bones and Burke had the same initials, and every time Bones readdressed the parcels

to Corney in the Mediterranean, they would come straight back to him. After 12 days based on Mulberry, temptation became too great for Bones. The two parcels were opened, a great feast was held, and next day the gourmands were back on compo-rations once more.

During the last days in Normandy there was little excitement for the flotilla. The boats still faced the same mine problem, but the shore batteries had fallen silent, and because enemy vessels were avoiding trouble (thank the Lord), patrols were almost dull.

Those furious days in the British Assault Area off Normandy, from 6 June 1944 until the first week in August, will be remembered forever by us all. The tense, exciting, yet grim experiences of war can never be wholly eradicated from our minds. Yet I think that we shall more often recall those cheerful characters who were bright and smiling even on the darkest days, and whose effervescent light-heartedness sustained the high morale of the flotilla, thus helping to pave the road to final victory. The Navy has always encouraged a keen sense of humour in its men, and this valuable quality marked the personnel of Coastal Forces. Never to be forgotten also are the great preparations for the invasion, and the equipment which had been designed especially for that gigantic operation. Now that the landings had succeeded and the liberation of France

begun, the exhausted 29th looked forward to many days of rest, days in which both craft and personnel could regain their strength, and with it the gay, happy spirit which had shone so brightly in the past.

CHAPTER SIX

REST FOR THE WEARY?

AFTER SEVEN DAYS OF SURVIVOR'S LEAVE, I found myself a terrified passenger on a flotilla motorcycle, whizzing down the main highway from Portsmouth to Hythe with Leading Stoker Powell, our dispatch rider, at the controls. I was on my way to deliver an address to the employees of British Power Boats at the request of the firm and to have a look at my new boat, MTB *486*. My nervousness concerning my speech was overshadowed by my fear for life and limb on this viciously bouncing vehicle. Nevertheless, we seemed to be doing fine, and Powell scoffed at my timidity. Then, not far from Hythe, we zoomed around a particularly sharp curve, and the motorcycle skidded out from under us and went sliding into the ditch. While Powell flew off in the opposite direction, I found myself slithering down the white line on the highway with legs and arms waving in the air. I felt extremely ridiculous, and was rather bruised in a certain spot. By the time I arrived at my destination some time later, I was a wreck.

The BP officials gave me a good drink to relieve my wounded dignity, but before long I was on the platform staring down at thousands of faces. Sure that they must be able to hear my knees knocking together, I began by thanking the people of British Power Boats for their magnificent co-operation during the invasion. Although their role had been far from glamorous, it had been extremely important. They had worked day and night to give the boats their 48-hour refits, as well as painting them with the compliments of the firm, and they were responsible for the fact that the 29th Flotilla had been able to maintain eight operational boats throughout the hectic early days of the landings in Normandy. Since the employees of BP had shown a great interest in the crews of the 29th and extended to many of them the hospitality of their homes, I told them as much as I could about the loss of *460*. I then closed my talk by thanking them from the bottom of my heart for the great work they had done in building such fine little fighting boats.

In early August, *486* was commissioned in true BP tradition, and then, accompanied by the rest of the flotilla (*485*, *461*, *462*, *464*, *465*, and *466*), she was on her way to Dover. The entire flotilla was headed for Ramsgate, which was under Dover Command, for a much-needed rest. Fitted forward of the bridge on *486* was its badge, a maple leaf, which had been carved from part of a 400-year-old oak beam from Warmwell House. Besides being the Canadian emblem, it held much sentimental value for me, for I had spent many pleasant off-duty hours at Warmwell House, and the carving itself had been on old *459*.

My new Motor Mechanic was Petty Officer Jim MacKay, who was older than the rest of us and possessed a charming personality and great understanding of human nature. He loved his new ship. Leading Stoker Brown was another new member of the crew. Stoker Roberts was the only surviving member of

Opposite: Aftereffects of a small party on an MTB. (PAC C127045)

The men of the 29th relax on Ramsgate Beach. (PAC C127037)

459's engine room crew. I had wanted him to go ashore for the rest he so badly needed, particularly since he was still suffering from the shock of the explosion, but he refused my offer because he preferred to remain with the ship's company of *459.*

The boats entered Ramsgate harbour and made fast alongside. HMCS *Canada,* the attractive barracks which the 29th had fixed up and had once called home, was now in the hands of the Polish Navy, so our men were given very unsatisfactory accommodation ashore, although it was the best the RN could offer. This resulted in only the pool ratings sleeping ashore, as the crews preferred to remain aboard their own boats. Every day when I inspected *486* I would see Jim MacKay, a sparkle in his eye, patting the boat with a fatherly touch, and I always felt that she really belonged to him.

The crew of *459/486* was a happy one; the boys got along well together and there was seldom any trouble. Life was pleasant at Ramsgate and the weather during our stay was glorious. In the mornings the men worked hard cleaning the ships, but in the afternoons they would have "make and mends". Officers and crews alike took full advantage of the sandy beach beneath the white cliffs, and after the weary, dreary days of Normandy, it was marvellous to relax and soak in the sunshine until we were all tanned to a handsome copper colour. Interspersed with bouts of sunbathing and refreshing dips in the cold, salty sea, the 29th often played baseball or American football on the hot sands. Then, around 1900 or 2000, a unit of boats would proceed to sea on the nightly patrol. Those who were not on duty would hire the decrepit taxi and drive over to Lucy's in Margate for a super meal, with a bottle of good white wine as the finishing touch.

After many months of struggling, our paymaster, Hal Ritchie, finally won a great victory. We were at last to get Canadian, rather than the smaller British rations; the crews could eat like kings. Hal had also managed an arrangement with the milkman, so we could regain a little of the weight lost during the fierce days in the Assault Area. At the same time, Irving Berlin convinced someone that our boats really did need a refit, and some were up on the slip almost immediately. All of them were badly in need of refitting, and since they were well past their 500 engine-hours, they were each due for three new engines. There was no rest for poor Irving; as soon as one job was finished, a new task took its place. But it was great for the crews to be able to take a bit of leave and have a spree in London. They always returned with smiles and empty pockets. Because the base at Ramsgate, HMS *Fervent,* did not have adequate facilities, the refits were not of a high standard, and were completed in a half-hearted manner. They were particularly disappointing as we had originally hoped to send our boats to BP for a good overhauling and re-engining, but this procedure had been impossible at the time.

Basil Ward, with a new half-stripe (making him a Lieutenant-Commander, RN), was Senior Officer of MTBs and was known as "the Fuhrer". I rang him up every day to report on the state of my boats and to find out what was cooking for the night's operation. Then we would break off into informal chatter about the recent highlights at the bases, and by the time we were ready to ring off both Basil and I were usually chuckling over the gossip.

Operations consisted mostly of anti-E-Boat patrols, which were invariably tedious. The boats of the 29th were usually placed in the middle of the Channel near South Varne Buoy, and the nights passed with hundreds of the V-1 doodlebugs flying overhead to London, intent on their destructive missions. One night in the month of August the shore batteries off Dungeness, manned by an American ack-ack unit, shot down 19 of 21 of these doodlebugs. The sight of the shells exploding against the blackness of the sky around the flying missiles was truly impressive. Eventually, a bubble of brilliant flame would appear, accompanied by a violent explosion and followed by a deathly silence. So ended another of the fluttering, sputtering doodlebugs. From time to time the shore batteries at Calais and Gris Nez bombarded Dover, 21 miles across the Strait, and in reply to the German challenge the Dover guns would awaken with an angry bark. The roaring of the guns and V-1s helped to relieve the monotony of the patrols and rescued us from the silence that usually prevailed save for the lapping of the waves against the boats. When the first rays of light began to warm the eastern sky after each patrol, the unit was only too glad to start its engines and set sail for Ramsgate.

These quiet patrols ended when the Allied armies swept like lightning across France. Tension ran high, the news was good, and nothing seemed to stop our troops. Panic-stricken Germans began to evacuate Le Havre, Fécamp, Dieppe, and other French ports, and activity in the Strait of Dover began to increase. The big guns of Calais roared unceasingly, spitting their venom on the little coastal towns. Dover itself received a terrible battering, and Deal and Ramsgate got a goodly share of the severe shelling. Every Allied convoy that passed through the Strait in daylight was enveloped in a smokescreen furnished by the tiny MA/SBs working from Ramsgate. The bombardment continued day and night until it almost seemed that the enemy was trying to get rid of his ammunition, for by this time Canadian troops were moving fast and furiously along the coast toward the heavy guns of Calais and Cap Gris Nez.

On the night of 20-21 August the Germans started to push some of their shipping through the Strait of Dover, under cover of their deadly shore batteries. Glen Creba and I, in *485* and *486* respectively, were lying out near the South Varne Buoy when Dover Castle vectored us north of Boulogne. Four German landing craft were sneaking through the Strait, keeping close to the cliffs. Our two MTBs surged through the black night at 30 knots. Visibility was not at its best, and it was a MacGoffoney night for radar. John Shand had a course well plotted for intercepting the nasty flak ships, which were similar to the ones we had attacked in the Strait of Dover back in May. In the meantime, Simpson was carrying out a careful radar sweep, and as we drew close to the enemy coast he picked up some echoes between Cap Gris Nez and Boulogne. Our unit altered course, and, increasing speed to 35 knots, we set off in the direction of the echoes. After a long chase we realized that they were only ironized MacGoffoneys. A second plot received from Dover placed the enemy north of us. In other words, he had passed us and was drawing away on a course opposite to our own. *485* and *486* altered course northward, and we adjusted our silencers to prevent giving away our position. Our boats ran at 35 knots on a course parallel to the shore, hoping to gain bearing on the four LCTs, which were known to be heavily armed with 88-mm, 37-mm, and 20-mm guns. Having passed Gris Nez without a shower from its accurate batteries, we ran up opposite Calais, where our radar picked up the enemy well inshore and running over a shallow sandbank which made it impossible to fire our torpedoes. They suddenly started firing starshells, and we counter-illuminated with the rockets fitted alongside our six-pounder gun. A brief exchange of gunfire took place, but the attack was abandoned when the enemy passed into the narrow Dunkirk channel. *486* and *485* resumed patrol position, highly annoyed with themselves for chasing ironized MacGoffoneys and thus ruining their attack. That morning, still disgusted, we sailed back to harbour.

Two evenings later we were again on patrol, and we found ourselves sitting on the ridge in the middle of the Strait of Dover listening to the doodlebugs sputtering overhead on their way to war-battered London. Intelligence had informed us that more enemy ships would be pulling out of Le Havre and Dieppe during the night and that they would proceed toward the Strait of Dover. The exact number of craft was not known, but it was certain that there would be 'M' class minesweepers, flak ships, R-Boats, and the old coasters, all of which would be laden with troops being evacuated from the various French ports. It was therefore planned that RAF Coastal Command aircraft would attack the convoy in the areas south of Boulogne and north of Calais as far as Dunkirk, while the MTBs would carry out their attack between Boulogne and Calais. Both air and sea forces would be controlled by radar from the Castle. At the appointed time the bombers began their mission well south of Boulogne, and I hoped that by the time the convoy reached our area it would be suffering from the shock of the Air Force blows and feeling a bit teased out. On this occasion *486, 461,* and *465* were accompanied by a Dutch flotilla of three MTBs, which were only lightly armed with small-calibre guns. We ourselves were really acting as MGBs, since each of our boats was armed with one six-pounder, power-driven, automatic gun and twin Oerlikons aft. Our unit was to cover and assist the Dutch boats should they become involved in a severe gun action, and we were also to aid in carrying out a torpedo attack.

South of Boulogne, and gradually drawing closer to it, I could see the German tracer attempting to inflict mortal wounds on the British bombers. The tracer ceased as the bombers flew away. A plot of the enemy's position was received every three minutes from Dover and carefully noted by John Shand. As the foe moved toward us, Dover ordered us to steer on an interception course at 20 knots. The Dutch flotilla took the lead, as arranged, and soon the enemy appeared on the radar scan. It was difficult to be sure at that moment how many vessels made up the convoy, but there seemed to be about 14. The Dutch boats formed up in Order 4, attack formation, while the 29th moved northward of them to leave plenty of room for the attack, and then we also moved into battle formation.

The two units closed the enemy, and when the range was 2,000 yards the Dutch MTBs started to illuminate with their rockets to seek out the torpedo targets, while we remained quiet and kept closing. For a few seconds the star-shells silhouetted the German convoy, showing us many small vessels ranging from 700 to 900 tons, which were mostly 'M' class minesweepers or flak trawlers. Then all hell broke loose. The enemy shore batteries had spotted us and opened up with all they had, and the guns of the evacuating German Army soon followed suit. The atmosphere was hot. With the range at 1,500 yards, *486,* Daddy Bones in *461,* and Chuff-Chuff in *465* simultaneously opened fire with our six-pounders. Our noisy rockets hurled themselves into the air, illuminating the convoy, and from where I stood on the bridge the noise was deafening. Ears buzzed and faces smarted from the blast of the six-pounder. The enemy was getting our range and both flotillas were being straddled. There was a steady roar of explosions. The Dutch disengaged and made smoke while we continued to move in, blazing away. At approximately 1,000 yards from the enemy ships we altered to Order 1. Our position was becoming exceedingly uncomfortable, and I knew that there was no point in sailing through the inferno, risking the loss of lives and boats, when it was almost certain we should not be able to collect a dividend. So the three boats of the 29th altered course 90°, made smoke to disengage, and zig-zagged their way out of the heavy barrage. Even after putting six miles between us and the shore batteries we were still being straddled, and it was useless to attack again because the enemy convoy was quickly nearing the bombing zone. Coastal Command would soon take over, dropping flares and bombs. In the morning we returned to base, harassed by lingering thoughts of the convoy and the shore batteries.

On 1 September a large operation was laid on by Dover Command. The 29th's officers, together with those of the RN, were briefed in the ancient castle. Intelligence had learned that at 2230, about five E-Boats would sail

Disengaging from heavily escorted convoy near Boulogne. (PAC C126988)

through the Strait of Dover. As our boats were the fastest and most heavily armed in the Command, Glen Creba and I were chosen to deal with these *Schnellboote* as the first phase of the operation. In the second phase the 29th was to return to No. 3 Buoy, join Basil Ward's flotilla, and carry out a zone torpedo attack north of Cap Gris Nez on approximately 14 evacuating craft ('M' class minesweepers and flak trawlers) that were sailing from Dieppe. This was to be a most interesting operation, as it involved all three services—aircraft, Dover shore batteries, and MTBs. The first aircraft were to bomb from Dieppe up to the Berk Buoy, Dutch MTBs were to attack well south of Boulogne, and the second group of bombers was to take care of the area from Boulogne as far as two miles south of Cap Gris Nez. From there the heavy Dover shore batteries would bombard up to Cap Blanc, and then the British MTBs commanded by Basil Ward, accompanied by the two boats of the 29th, would attack from Cap Blanc to Calais. Well north of Calais the third group of bombers would carry out their mission to Dunkirk. This convoy, incidentally, was to be the last, as the Canadian Army was on the outskirts of all the German ports south of Boulogne.

At 2205 Glen and I joined Basil Ward's four boats at the rendezvous, No. 3 Buoy, where we stopped and waited for further orders from Dover. The men, knowing what they could expect at any moment, were tense with excitement. At 2212 orders came for me to steer 135° for nine miles at 30 knots, a course that would take us under those horrible Cap Gris Nez shore batteries. Basil Ward shouted across to us, "Best of luck to you, Tony and Glen," and then *486* and *485* moved off, gathering speed until we were planing at the required 30 knots. The sea was quite rough and the boats crashed from one wave to another as they swept toward Gris Nez. Visibility was marvellous; we could see for miles, and the moon, sitting right over the Cape, was in our favour. The chalk-white cliffs of the French coast grew closer, and at 2224 Simpson picked up radar contacts bearing Green 20, 1,400 yards, amplitude 2x. *486* and *485* altered course and opened fire, but due to the rough seas our six-pounders jammed. There we were, 1,000 yards from the enemy and still closing, with only our silly little .303 machine-guns piffing away, merely tickling the E-Boats. To bring the Oerlikons to bear on the enemy, *486* went hard a-starboard toward the enemy and then ran on a parallel course. It almost seemed that I would ram one of the E-Boats as I turned 180° and closed to 100 yards or less. The twin Oerlikons opened up and were soon joined by the cleared six-pounders of both boats, so that the fleeing enemy were being subjected to a good barrage. The engagement took place at almost point-blank range, but fortunately the enemy's guns replied in only a half-hearted manner, while we managed to do a goodly share of damage to the *Schnellboote.* Finally the E-Boats made smoke, and at their maximum speed ran for Calais harbour.

The twin 20-mm Oerlikon was the after-armament on the 29th's MTBs. (PAC PA144581)

The best we could do was 41 knots. Nevertheless, both MTBs kept firing into the smoke hoping to hit something. Amazingly enough, as the E-Boats approached Calais breakwater the batteries opened up with green and yellow tracer, and gave them a rousing welcome with 20- and 37-mm shells. The surprised *Schnellboote* had to fire all sorts of recognitions into the air before the shore batteries realized their error. Our two boats, their six-pounders still firing, were now about a mile from the mouth of Calais harbour, and as I looked up at the towering white cliffs of Gris Nez I was thoroughly frightened by the idea that the shore batteries were probably peering down on us and taking careful aim. With intense relief I watched the cliffs diminish in size as we planed away over the bumpy sea. *486* and *485* rejoined the British MTBs, and in the ensuing lull we caught our breath while Basil welcomed us back with words of praise. Although the two boats had come out of the action with only superficial damage, we had suffered two casualties. Ordinary Seaman Belliveau, the No. 3 on the six-pounder, had had one arm badly hurt by the recoil on the gun and was in great pain. William Dublack, an Oerlikon gunner, better known in *486* as "Dublack the Killer", had been hit by a shell splinter which had cut into his shoe and nicked one of his toes. It was not terribly painful, but he was extremely annoyed with the enemy for having had the nerve to shoot in his direction.

At 2330 we moved off, and were ordered to stop and wait in a position seven miles off Cap Gris Nez. To the south we could see Hans Larive and his Dutchmen battling it out with the evacuating convoy. When Hans had completed his engagement, the second group of bombers came in and did their part, and after Coastal Command had ended their mission the most dramatic and noisy phase of the plan came into action. The Dover shore batteries opened up with mighty flashes, and shells started to crash around the remaining harassed enemy boats. I didn't envy them. I saw one direct hit on what looked like a flak trawler, which blew up and disappeared. German shore batteries, meanwhile, had answered the challenge and were spitting out brilliant flashes followed by angry barks, and all the while our unit, sitting between the duellists, had an eye-witness view of the whole show. It was like sitting in the middle of the ring during a championship boxing match—the sensation was phenomenal. Shells continued to crash around the shattered convoy, sending up huge water-spouts, while shells from the German batteries rained down on Dover.

Then came our cue. We were ordered to attack, and the unit moved off in Order 4. *486* moved off too, but in a self-chosen direction—her steering had gone. So only Glen Creba continued with Basil for the zone attack with torpedoes, while *486* remained behind, her company steeped in disappointment. Jim MacKay went through the system with a fine-toothed comb, and he finally found that a pin had dropped out of the steering in a most awkward spot, the petrol-tank compartment. MacKay worked like a fiend to repair the defect. I was completely exasperated with *486,* for I had been very anxious to get in on the last phase of the magnificent operation.

As soon as the boats had been noticed, both the shore batteries and the convoy opened up on the five MTBs, making it most unpleasant for them. The unit fired their torpedoes together in a zone attack. One enemy ship blew up and sank. Satisfied with their contribution, the MTBs turned away together and disengaged behind a smokescreen, which was most welcome because the heavy batteries above the Cape were straddling the unit with everything they had. Finally the third bomber group flew in to give the enemy more punishment, and I couldn't help but pity our battered foe, as I thought he had had enough. It was later learned that only five of the original 14 boats reached Ostend and that the crews of these had understandably been severely shaken. The combined operation had gone like clockwork, smoothly and efficiently, and it had been a fine example of teamwork among the three services.

We arrived back at the base in the morning feeling more than a little annoyed with *486,* although, of course, no one could be blamed for the accident. It was just one of those unforeseen things that can happen. I was particularly sorry for Chief Petty Officer MacKay, who felt that the breakdown of the steering had been his fault. But I managed to coax him back into good spirits and by the time I left the boat he was smiling again.

Back in my fourth-floor room at the Yacht Club, I found two letters awaiting me. The first one I opened contained a blast from NSHQ for having had a slight collision at Holyhead with my old friend Kirkpatrick, away back in April when we were all working up. I was really down in the dumps after reading it. It certainly wasn't the type of thing I needed after the disappointment of our night's work. After a moment I picked up the other letter with a sigh. Written in flowery and beautiful English, it stated that the King had graciously awarded me the Distinguished Service Cross. Needless to say, this made me feel much better. So a kick in the pants and a pat on the back constituted my welcome for that morning.

After a wash and breakfast I went down to the Flotilla Office, where I was pleased to see in the AFOs that Leading Seaman William Reid, Able Seaman Bushfield, and Ordinary Seaman William Dublack, all of *459/486,* had each received the Distinguished Service Medal, and that Able Seaman James Wright of *466* had been given the same award. It was a great day for the boys. Also on the list of awards was the name of Ordinary Seaman Frederick Thompson Armstrong, late of MTB *464,* who had received a posthumous Mention in Despatches, the citation for which read: "For gallantry, skill, determination and undaunted devotion to duty during the initial landing of the Allied forces on the Coast of Normandy."

One day a fellow by the name of Nick Reid blew down to Ramsgate from London with all kinds of cameras and related equipment. The 29th Flotilla was about to break into the movies. It was quite an undertaking for Nick to fit his plans in with operational requirements. He persuaded the Royal Marines to fix up an old hull to look like an E-Boat, and this contraption was towed out on the "set". Following shouts of "Camera!", the flotilla would roar in and shoot up the hulk, only to hear the cry, "Cut! Cut! Do that over again." Again and again we roared in, trying to sink this wooden hulled E-Boat. We blasted it with all our six-pounders and Oerlikon guns, we set demolition charges, we fired everything we could think of to sink the damned thing, but all we managed to do was to send splinters flying about. Many weeks went into the making of this film, which, when completed, was called *Sea Fleas.*

Kirkpatrick and his flotilla sailed into Dover harbour one evening, and we received an invitation to visit them. All the officers of the 29th who could be mustered at the moment climbed aboard the flotilla truck, and our driver steamed down the narrow highway to Dover. After receiving a royal welcome from Kirkie and his officers, we all climbed down an oily ladder to *748,* Ollie Mabee's boat. Between drinks Kirkie related the story of one of their successful actions near St. Malo. It seemed that they had attacked a German convoy, sinking two merchant ships, setting one escort vessel ablaze, and damaging several others, but Kirkie assured us that outside of these incidents, the "do" had been extremely quiet.

Basil Ward and Pluggie were in on the party that night, the only two British officers among the boisterous Canadians. Ollie Mabee was in a loquacious mood and kept getting up every few minutes to make a speech, but Les McLernon, his Number One, had only to put his hand on Ollie's shoulder and he would quickly sit down again. Kirk's flotilla was *en route* to Great Yarmouth, their new base, but they would also be working from Ostend, where Daddy Brind's CFMU 1 was shortly to be assigned. It was good to see Kirkie and his boys again, and after a very fine party it was with much regret that we finally bade them farewell and returned to Ramsgate. I never did find out what Ollie Mabee had wanted to say.

One day I drove to Dover to see Basil Ward, and found the streets of the little town jammed with celebrating crowds, while Union Jacks fluttered from the wreckage of their shattered homes. All the shops were closed, but the pubs were open and the people of Dover were enjoying themselves to the hilt. Their

Opposite and next page: The larger, slower, but more heavily armed D-class MTBs of the other Canadian MTB flotilla, the 65th. (PAC PA144584, PA144585)

gaiety was understandable, for the Calais shore batteries had been captured by the Canadians. The final bombardment of Dover had lasted well over a hundred hours, and had destroyed the homes of many of the people who now made up the happy, laughing crowds. By afternoon the throngs were roaming the streets arm-in-arm, singing at the tops of their voices. Most of them had been celebrating all day and by this time were feeling no pain, and I noticed that even some of the dogs were barely able to navigate.

At the end of several dull weeks we received four spare officers, all midshipmen whose respective names were Ireland, Sabiston, Howard, and Hobarth, and who were soon nick-named "Red Snoots". Ireland came to *486*, Howard to *461*, Hobarth to *464*, and Sabiston to *465*, replacing Barney Marshall, who had been wounded back in Normandy. Dick Paddon, Creba's Number One, came to my boat to replace John. Another new arrival was "Irish" Martin, so-called because of his pronounced accent, who went to Creba's boat as Number One. The "Red Snoots" were very pleased to be in MTBs, and proved to be keen, efficient officers. They were quick to catch on to their various duties, and soon even became adept in handling the boats and bringing them alongside the jetty. It was unfortunate that they had come to us during a lull, when it seemed there would be no more excitement in the Strait of Dover. Boulogne and Calais had fallen, and the Canadian Army had by-passed Dunkirk to take Ostend, where Daddy Brind had established his Mobile Coastal Force Unit. At this time it looked as if the war was likely to end very soon, for nothing seemed able to stop the Allied armies.

I received a signal from CNMO advising me that the Senior Canadian Naval Padre, Bishop Wells, accompanied by Padre Foote, was going to visit us. Suitable accommodation was scarce, so I thought Bishop Wells might like my tiny room. It was small, but its windows afforded a lovely view of the harbour. Several of my paintings hung on the wall, lending the room a little colour. On Saturday evening I met them at the station and saw to it that they were made comfortable. The next morning was beautiful, and everyone looked very smart at Divisions. After the Captain of HMS *Fervent* had completed his inspection, Divine Service was held. Padre Foote conducted the service and Bishop Wells delivered the sermon. The latter was a very stately clergyman, and the many ribbons on his tunic denoting service in the Boer War and the two Great Wars indicated that he was well into his seventies. His sermon was simple, human, and full of understanding, and received much favourable comment from the British Naval officers present, many of whom said it was the finest they had ever heard. It is a pity that we did not have more like it. After the service I invited the Bishop and Padre Foote for a quick trip to sea in *486*. The water was rough as we left the harbour and roared out through a convoy. Bishop Wells greatly enjoyed the trip despite the somewhat high seas, and indeed appeared quite stimulated by the stiff breeze. When we returned, Captain Howard, RN (NOIC Ramsgate) joined us on board for a quiet sherry, after which our two guests departed for London.

The Dutch flotillas had all paid off, and in honour of the occasion they threw a terrific dinner party in the pens at Dover. They called the dinner a *rijsttafel* (rice table), and many days of preparation were necessary to make ready the repast, which was cooked aboard the pens and MTBs. The Admiral and his staff and many Coastal Force characters, including Bobby Moyse and myself, were on hand to bid farewell to Hans Larive and his comrades. Since the fall of Holland they had fought side by side with us, and we were all sorry to see them go.

The dinner itself was magnificent, and fascinatingly unfamiliar. Each person received a very large plate, in the centre of which was a mound of rice. This was the foundation for the 16 artistically arranged dishes that followed. We took a small helping of each of these delicious-looking concoctions, which together entirely filled up our plates. Beer was served to wash down the meal, which was hot and spicy, suggestive of Dutch East Indian food. A menu had been provided, but it meant little to most of us, for it read like this:

Rijsttafel

Nassi
Ikan – Goreng
Kerry
Sajoeran Manis
Sajoeran Pedis
Ketimoen Adjar
Rotmok
Ati – Goreng
Pricadel
Ajam Goreng Bali
Ajam Goreng Pedis
Kentang Goreng
Sajoeran Lombok
Daging Babi
Daging Kantjing
Sambal Bawan

Marietja – Lombok – Garem – Adjar – Moster

. . . .

Boeah – Bosah

After finishing this massive meal scarcely anyone could move, for our ration-trained stomachs were not used to such a quantity of food. At the conclusion of the dinner several amusing speeches, which included much leg-pulling, were given by the Admiral and his staff. The cook was called for, and when that Dutch seaman appeared, he was greeted with well-earned cheers from the assembled company, and thanks and congratulations from the Admiral. Then Hans Larive said good-bye to us all and thanked the Royal Navy for its kindness and co-operation. Most of us left early, with well fed drowsiness.

Poor Able Seaman Parks of *462* had by this time undergone nearly 18 operations, and it was thanks to one of the best doctors in England that he was alive at all. Admiral Nelles wrote to let me know he had seen the lad, and assured me that he was receiving the best of care. The Admiral certainly took a great interest in the welfare of the two Canadian flotillas and their crews. I sent Parks's brother off to Gosport on two weeks' leave so he could cheer up his twin at Haslar Hospital.

The day came when those seamen who had defaulted from duty were to be passed under review. The Captain of the base stood sternly behind a green table, with several other officers, including myself, behind. After considering the cases of the defaulters, a seaman who looked familiar to me was brought before the Captain. The Chief Petty Officer ordered "Off Caps" and the Petty Officer turned to the Captain and read the charge: "Able Seaman Deschêsnes, Sir [smart salute], was absent over leave, namely seven hours 14 minutes, and failed to report aboard his boat HMC MTB *461.*"

The Captain addressed Deschêsnes in a quiet, sympathetic voice, "You know your boat is operational?"

"Yes, Sir."

"This is a rather serious matter; what have you got to say?"

Deschêsnes immediately burst into a long explanation, his French and his English becoming more mixed up the further he went. "Well, Sir, it was dis way, Sir. I-I was in de station of Veectoria an' I 'ad a few minute so I 'ad a small beer. Well, den it was time for de train to go an' I run like anyting down de platform wid de gasmask an' de satchel an' I go on de train as she pull out from de station. After going long time somebody she say dis train she doesn't go to Ramsgate, she go to Seven Hoaks. *Mon Dieu,* [hands flying in the air] dis was de wrong train! I climbs off and into anudder train. I find dis train she only go to Canterbury so I gets off at Canterbury in disgust. I decide to go to anudder pub and haf a drink to tink things over. After a time I realize she is *très* tired—I fall off my seat—my gasmask she gets caught wid de seat an' I loose my keys an' satchel—everything is *très* bad. After a terrible time I arrive at Ramsgate *sept heures et quatorze minutes* late and I'm terribly sorry, Sir."

At the end of this recitation the bewildered Captain hemmed and hawed and finally mumbled something about Number Eleven. The Petty Officer named the punishment in his cockney accent and then ordered, "On caps, about turn and double march."

As soon as Deschêsnes had doubled out of the room, the Captain, still looking very doubtful, bent over and whispered in my ear, "Actually, Law, I didn't understand one word that man said." That was the end of defaulters for that day.

The MTB officers were continually being shifted about, creating no little confusion. John and Footsie went down to BP to recommission *459,* which would soon be ready. She had been towed back to England in August, coming dangerously close to sinking on the way. The repairs had cost about twice as much as the original price of the boat. Daddy Bones had left with his ship's company to commission *491,* one of the new type of boats similar to *486* and *485.* My First Lieutenant, Dick Paddon, was given command of MTB *466.* To replace him on *486,* my boat, a new officer by the name of MacBeth was posted in. One of the "Red Snoots", Midshipman Ireland, was my Third Officer. Scobie was given command of *461,* Daddy Bones's old boat, and his First Lieutenant was Bill Hale, also a newcomer. Poor old Scobie had a very green crew.

On 13-14 September, *486, 466,* and *485* were ordered to carry out a patrol a little north of Dunkirk, to stop enemy E-Boats which were supplying the German army still holding the city. It was a difficult mission, as we had to proceed off Calais and up the treacherously narrow channel of Dunkirk, and I kidded MacBeth about the navigation of which he was so confident. It was a long trip up the channel, and the boats glided quietly through the water at ten knots, with silencers. The three craft had almost arrived at Dunkirk when, seeing a white surf and hearing the waves breaking on the shore, I ordered the unit to stop. The harbour was only about 500 yards ahead of us, and I thought we were too close to the shore and off the Channel. The boats altered to seaward, and just at that moment the enemy switched on a searchlight a mere 400 yards away. I was sure the end had come. Our boats were surrounded by steel obstructions, placed there by the Germans to prevent landings on the beach. Glen Creba in *485* hit some of these wretched things with his propellers, and so did *486.* Both boats vibrated terribly. Disengaging slowly under the powerful sweep of the searchlight, we all held our breaths, hoping against hope that the batteries on the breakwater wouldn't open up. Luck was with us that night, and we managed to tiptoe away safely. Next morning *486* and *485* slipped for new propellers, and we all thanked God that we weren't having breakfast as prisoners-of-war in Dunkirk.

The following night, 15-16 September, the same operation was laid on for *486, 462, 485,* and *465,* and we all breathed a sigh of relief when it was cancelled due to bad weather. Nevertheless, the same assignment was handed to us the next night, with *464* replacing *485.* Everything went according to plan as the four MTBs, taking no chances this time, proceeded up the Channel to Dunkirk. We had almost reached our destination when Dover signalled us to return to harbour. We could see no reason for this order, as the radar was clear and the weather was good, but we dutifully turned around, and after several hours of steaming we reached the base. I immediately rang up the Senior Officer Operations to ask why the boats had been sent out only to be recalled, and received the astounding reply, "You should be thankful we recalled you in time. Intelligence reported that the enemy had laid mines across the narrow channel off Dunkirk harbour, and had also set floating traps and other obstructions." We rang off, and I turned grateful eyes to the heavens and said a silent prayer of thanks.

After these two frightening events, patrols became very dull. Religiously we went to Nieuport Bank Buoy, situated between Dunkirk and Ostend, every night. The monotony was slightly relieved on 1 October, when *462* and *464* illuminated Dunkirk harbour and fired some shells on the town, receiving a lone German starshell in acknowledgment. The show had been given for the benefit of three gentlemen representing the Victory Loan, who wanted something exciting to tell the Canadian people to stimulate the sale of bonds. Each night as we lay out at Nieuport Bank Buoy, we could hear old Kirkie, who was north of us near Ostend, saying, "Calling all cars . . . calling all cars. This is Kirkie. Order 1 . . . Order 1. I say again, Order 1 . . . go . . . go . . . go. Over." It was good to hear Canadian voices over the air.

On 3 October *486* and *466,* which was once again commanded by Barney Marshall, proceeded to Ostend with the same three gentlemen on board. Jack Nichols, one of the Official Naval War Artists, was also with us looking for interesting subject matter. After lunching with Daddy Brind in Ostend, we left the Victory Loan representatives safe in the hands of the Army and returned to Ramsgate.

On 8 October *486* was put up on the slip to allow Reid, Bushfield, and Dublack to attend the investiture at Buckingham Palace. They were accompanied by Wright of *466,* and each was permitted to take two guests. There was scarcely anyone left to man *486,* and the only solution to the problem was to temporarily slip the dear old girl.

On 21 October, the 29th Flotilla was ordered to sail to HMS *Beehive* at Felixstowe, which was commanded by Commander T. Kerr. Daddy Bones's wife and my sister-in-law both came down to say goodbye to us, as they would be on their way to Canada before we returned. *486* was laden with all sorts of equipment, including the CO's bicycle, as she led the way out of Ramsgate harbour followed by *491*, *462*, *485*, *466*, and *461*. *465* remained behind for a refit. The people of the town turned out to wave us goodbye, and many were tearful, for some of our sailors were leaving their new brides. Ramsgate soon faded from sight, and the boats pushed on across the Thames Estuary to the East Coast on their way to Felixstowe, which was under the command of Commander-in-Chief, Nore.

Opposite: On our way to patrol. (PAC C127019)

CHAPTER SEVEN

ANTICLIMAX

THE COASTAL FORCE BASE at Felixstowe, HMS *Beehive,* was tightly efficient, and in no time had carried out excellent refits on the boats. Each craft, sitting on a cradle with wheels, was simply towed out of the water by tractors and into the huge hangar which had been handed over to Coastal Force by the RAF. There were two Officers' Messes, one in the Pier Hotel near the dock, where all the Senior Officers were billeted, and the other in Felixstowe, five miles from the base. The houses which had contained the RAF married quarters in peacetime were allotted to the crews, one house per boat, and these pleasant modern homes formed quite a community centre. The Canadian crews were later moved to what had been a large convalescent home run by a Canadian regulating staff, and was now known as HMCS *Canada II.*

Coastal Force operations under C-in-C Nore were engaged in three types of work. One group of Motor Launches and 'D' class MTBs constituted what was called 'Z' line, a patrol line extending five miles east of the convoy route from the mouth of thc Thamcs cstuary to 25 miles past Great Yarmouth. This was purely a defensive line, and it soon became known as the "Zizz" line, because during the monotonous and sleepy patrol one did practically nothing except adjust position hourly. A second patrol line, designed to protect the convoy routes to Antwerp, stretched from the Thames estuary across to the Scheldt, 25 miles north of Ostend, and it consisted of frigates, destroyers, and MTBs. The frigates were again American-built Destroyer Escorts (DEs) manned by the Royal Navy. They served as control ships, each frigate controlling one destroyer and two groups of MTBs, two of which craft made up a group.

The third operation, *Bangor,* was designed to seek out and destroy enemy shipping. This periodic sweep along the German convoy route started at the Hook of Holland, took in Ijmuiden, Texel, and Terschelling, and went as far north as the mouth of the Ems River. The first weeks of the operation were disheartening, for the winter weather had begun. Following the frigate and destroyer we would set out to patrol and guard the life-line to Belgium. The winds would then blow up to gale force, and we would be forced to slog our way back to harbour, arriving soaking and cold. Along with patrols we participated in a strenuous training programme; both "Tactical Teacher" and "Tactical Plot" were on the agenda twice a week, and we also had two gunnery shoots a week. W/T exercise took place every morning and we had to take part in one night encounter, with radar, and make dummy torpedo attacks on the Harwich destroyers.

The flotilla quickly settled into the routine, and at the end of our first week we were promised a *Bangor* operation. Our friend Peter Scott was now Senior Officer Operations for Coastal Force on the Nore Command's Staff, and he laid on a *Bangor* for 30 October. *486, 485, 491,* and *464* were briefed and

Opposite: MTB 486. (C.A. Law)

all boats were made ready, but at the last moment the operation was cancelled because of bad weather. That same day, old *459* recommissioned at British Power Boats, Poole, with John Shand as Supreme Fuhrer and Footsie as Number One. The operation having been scrubbed, we all went ashore to celebrate the good news, heading for "Fuggers", our favourite pub in Felixstowe. This was the rendezvous point for many Coastal Force types, and on almost every evening a group could be heard going through their large repertoire of gay and somewhat risqué songs.

Next day, 1 November, Peter Scott rang up to inform us that the 29th Flotilla would be required that night for a *Bangor.* Intelligence had reported much enemy shipping off the Hook of Holland and approximately 30 E- and R-Boats at Ijmuiden. An Allied landing had therefore been scheduled for 1 and 2 November on Walcheren Island in the Scheldt Estuary, south of the Hook of Holland. The tactical objective was to capture the shore batteries and drive the enemy from the north side of the Scheldt as far as Antwerp Estuary. This accomplished, the Allies would be able to use Antwerp harbour to land supplies for their armies. That gallant, battle-scarred old lady, the *Warspite,* was to support the landing forces with her heavy guns. Peter concluded by saying, "At all costs the 29th is to stop any E- or R-Boats proceeding southward."

In the first division were MTBs *486, 485,* and Scobie's boat, *461,* and the second division was made up of *491* and *464.* All five boats moved slowly out of the small Felixstowe harbour, saluting the Commanding Officer of *Beehive* as he bade them farewell, and then for many long hours we battled the cold, dirty North Sea. The wind was at least Force 5, nearly gale force. Scobie's engine began complaining, and eventually *461* was forced to drop out. Scobie was badly disappointed, but it was impossible to effect engine repairs on the spot.

Four boats were left to push their way to the Hook of Holland. The moon was high over the area of the Dutch coast—unfavourable for us, since it acted as a permanent starshell and ensured visibility for a good eight or nine miles. At 1931 my binoculars picked out minute black shapes leaving the Hook of Holland and heading northward close inshore. They were picked up by our radar at a range of seven miles. I ordered the unit to go into Order 4, battle formation; we would close the enemy together. Our four boats crept in slowly, hoping for a surprise torpedo attack, and as the silhouettes grew they were identified as several flak trawlers, one merchant ship of about 3,000 tons, a gun coaster, and a barge being towed by a tug. Everything was going fine; our speed was ten knots and the enemy hadn't spotted us. Suddenly, to the south of us and running on a collision bearing, appeared several E- or R-Boats, which were bearing down rapidly. Glen Creba and I altered course to southward and proceeded to engage the seven enemy boats in a fierce action. Our two boats returned everything they received; guns were blazing broadside and the gunners were doing magnificent work. We ran all the way down the long line of enemy boats, and all hell broke loose when the convoy opened up as well. Daddy Bones and Bish sighted the merchant ship and closed, though they were heavily straddled by the enemy. At 700 yards Daddy Bones fired his two torpedoes, which splashed heavily into the water and then ran true with a shallow setting. When Bones saw them they were well on their way. No one in the MTBs felt the explosion, but all of them saw a terrific, blinding flash before a large pall of ink-black smoke belched into the sky. Bish was unable to send off his torpedoes because his boat had been hit below the water line and gallons of water had flooded the mess deck. A second shell had instantly killed Able Seaman Harry Broadly and slightly wounded Able Seaman Allan Bevan. Bish might not have made it home again if Petty Officer Motor Mechanic F.A. Walden hadn't used his initiative and made a tingle against the hole with a large board, a submariner's white sweater, and a sawed-off boat hook. With these wedged in place, *464* was seaworthy again; the water could be pumped out of the mess deck and she could continue, thanks to Walden. Meanwhile, Bones and Bish had disengaged through the enemy screen on the opposite side of the convoy.

MTBs *486* and *485* had given the seven E- and R-Boats a hearty welcome, and vice versa. Both Glen's boat and mine got in some good hits, and it looked as if one of the enemy craft was on fire. We altered course toward the convoy and went in for a torpedo attack, but unfortunately we were spotted and illuminated. Our attempt thwarted, we charged with a violent gun action. 88-mm shells were soon bursting about our two craft while green and yellow tracers rained down in torrents. Our unit closed, trying to knock out one of the enemy escorts, but the flak was so violent and furious that we had to disengage, having only succeeded in wounding our victim. The enemy convoy made a 180° turn and went back to their starting-point, the Hook of Holland.

By means of their fighting lights Daddy Bones and Bish rejoined Glen and myself, and we nattered excitedly over the RT. There was nothing for it but that Bish's badly damaged boat would have to go back to harbour. Calling to Bish over the loud-hailer, I told him that he'd better have another boat escort him home, but he replied that he could return under his own steam and with this he departed. Daddy Bones, Glen, and I had pulled up our socks and reloaded our guns when we sighted what appeared to be a sailboat just south of the Hook of Holland. As we closed this object our boats seemed to be riding a peculiar swell, and were behaving as though they were in shallow water. Dick Paddon switched on the echo sounder. The reading was eight feet of water. We rapidly turned to get out of our precarious position, and discovered at the same time that our "sailboat" was a Dutch windmill.

The coxswain tapped me on the shoulder, "Don't look now, but I think we're being followed." Turning to see who our friends were, I was amazed to find the notorious Four Horsemen, a German patrol of four flak trawlers. Although I hadn't come in contact with these uncouth gentlemen since 1943 when I had been working off the Dutch coast, I knew that these bullies were far from gentle and that no matter what was done they would always get the upper hand, especially on a moonlit night. We spent the remainder of the night playing a game with each other which consisted mainly of batting shells back and forth. No one was getting hurt, but it was a frighteningly dangerous game. As soon as we had manoeuvred into a possible torpedo position and were ready to pull the lever, what would happen? The Four Horsemen would alter course toward us, and just to keep the game lively they would slam out a few more 88-mms. Later on we discovered something which was very embarrassing to both teams: the Four Horsemen and ourselves had been assigned to the same patrol position. The game went on; at the end of the period there was still no score and the flak trawlers and our three boats changed sides. They went to the southern end of the patrol while we took up our position at the northern end, and all the while we eyed each other and dreamed up new defensive plays. This battle reminded me of a hockey match.

Simpson then picked up four echoes to the north of us sailing down at 20 knots. They scared the pants off us by straddling us from five miles away. Our three boats disengaged at high speed on a westerly course, leaving the Four Horsemen to the south, and after proceeding on this course for several miles we stopped. I could hear Kirkpatrick, north of us, nattering over the air, and his outfit seemed to be getting a hot reception from the heavily armed 'M' class minesweepers whose shells were straddling them at approximately six miles. One direct hit caused severe damage to one of Kirk's boats.

We returned to our patrol, and having decided to take the initiative we crossed the blue line to engage the Horsemen once more. Our offensive play was well met, for they replied with heavy and accurate gunfire, keeping their bows toward us. After a time they apparently became bored with that, for they turned their sterns to us. By this time, 0315, *486, 491,* and *485* were running low on ammunition, and we decided to retain what was left in case enemy E-Boats tried to break through down toward the south. A short while later we thought we had sighted several E-Boats, and began a chase, until we discovered, to our embarrassment, that they were Allied boats.

At 0430 in the morning, in compliance with our orders, we left our patrol and headed for home. A stiff wind was blowing from the west, and our three boats received quite a pounding. Nevertheless, it wasn't long before we sighted a friendly buoy, and we were soon within viewing distance of Cork light vessel. We raced by her at top speed to see who could get to the fuelling jetty first, and we put up such a large wake in the scramble that I am sure the skipper of the boom defence vessel must have been knocked out of his bunk. The boats made fast alongside at approximately the same time, and there was a mad rush for the petrol hoses, of which there were two large ones and one small one. Captain Kerr was there to greet us. It never seemed to matter what time we came in—even in the wee small hours—the Captain of *Beehive* was always down to see his boys in. This welcome was practically a tradition at Felixstowe. It wasn't long before I had climbed into a lovely hot bath, and later I slowly came back to life and a beautiful plate of bacon and eggs.

Time went on and there were more patrols at sea. With the approach of winter everyone grew colder and wetter, and finally it seemed that no matter how much clothing I put on I was always frozen before the night was out. Weighted down by my clothes, I found breathing difficult, and I usually felt like a stuffed duck as I climbed aboard. One day while dressing for sea, I noticed my electric suit hanging on a hook in the cupboard. It was actually an RAF flying suit I had bought for the sum of one pound from a Naval officer on the Motor Anti-Submarine Boat (MA/SB) at Ramsgate. Divesting myself of all my extra garments, I climbed into the electric suit, and in this ridiculous garb, with the long attachment cord wound round my arm, I went down to *486*. I asked MacKay if it would be all right to use the Aldis light socket on the bridge, and then, much to the amusement of the crew, I plugged myself in.

MTB *486* sailed out of harbour with the boats following behind in close station-keeping. I had never felt so comfortable, for although the suit was comparatively light, it was cosy and warm. By the time we arrived at our patrol position the weather was deteriorating, so all units were ordered to return to harbour. Despite the weather, the Senior Officer was very warm indeed; in fact, I had never before enjoyed a trip so much. We were crashing our way back to Felixstowe when *486* hit a colossal wave, and gallons of water poured over the bridge. There was a dancing blue flash, and all the lights in the boat blinked out. My beautiful electric suit had shorted . . . and I was drenched. The unit entered Felixstowe with one boat minus its steaming lights, the culprit being *486*. Chiefie took a very dim view of the whole experiment, so after the suit had spent many days drying it was promptly put up for sale. That was the end of my electric suit.

Most of the boats had been refitted before Glen Creba's turn came to slip with *485*. The entire crew and CO all went on leave, which apparently turned out to be very pleasant indeed. When Glen entered the Flotilla Office upon his return this fact was written all over his face. His eyes, sparkling like diamonds, didn't seem to be able to focus on any object. Sitting on the edge of my desk and gazing at the ceiling with a rapt expression, he sighed. "When is my next slipping? It must be soon . . . I'm in love. Just can't tell you how lovely she is."

Dhobeying (wash day). (PAC C127036)

Anxious to be of assistance to him in this happy hour I looked up the slipping programme, only to find that *485* would not be slipped for the next three months. I assured the poor boy that we would try to fit him in at the earliest possible moment so that he could see his love again, and with that Glen simply floated out of the office grinning beatifically.

A *Bangor* off the Hook of Holland was slated for 23-24 December. Since *486* was on leave at this time, Daddy Bones was acting Senior Officer, and was accompanied on this occasion by *491, 465, 464, 485, 466, 459,* and *461.* This was the largest number of the 29th's MTBs that had ever sailed together on an offensive operation. Unfortunately, John Shand had to turn back because of a slight collision, which occurred through no fault of his own. The remaining six boats patrolled off the Hook of Holland throughout the night, but things remained quiet and not a single E-Boat was sighted.

On 31 December the 29th had but one operational boat; for some unknown reason the others had all chosen to break down together. The Senior Officer was also in drydock with an attack of the flu. My disease, which was accompanied by much sneezing and wheezing, had no doubt been given an extra boost by the overzealous leave which had preceded it. So the old year was gasping its last breath without me, and at Felixstowe harbour the arrival of the successor was being heralded by the firing of two star cartridges.

Our friend Bobby Moyse was at the Felix Hotel for the occasion, and was in magnificent form. George and Dragon ran the bar: George, a dignified, quiet, and extremely polite fellow was in charge; and Dragon was the second-in-command. Dragon was a rather formidable-looking woman, but this was merely a blind concealing a heart of gold. Her nickname had been affectionately bestowed upon her by the Coastal Force because she always wore a small green dragon pin on her dress, and because she had the very thoughtful habit of accidentally locking us in the bar after closing hours. At such times a great sing-song would usually develop, with Dragon rendering her favourite song, "Come daisies, come buttercups, q-u-a-c-k, q-u-a-c-k."

On this New Year's Eve, "The Moyse" was feeling no pain, and although there was a great deal of noise in the bar and he was asking for a drink in his most subdued voice, it still echoed throughout the room. An official-looking gentleman wearing a smart tweed sports jacket approached Bobby and quietly asked him to refrain from making so much racket. The Moyse turned to this dignified person, gave a supercilious stare, and pronounced, "My name is J. Wimpey Moyse and I'll make as much damn noise as I please." Some time later, when Bobby learned that the restraining influence on his boisterous good spirits was a rather senior captain in the Royal Navy, needless to say, he was a bit concerned.

The New Year's party ended with the Dragon's "Come daisies, come buttercups," which she occasionally interrupted with, "Time, ladies and gentlemen, please."

One night early in the New Year, *486* and *485* were returning from patrol in a very thick fog aided by the marvellous new radar set fitted in *486,* the only one of its kind in Coastal Force. Closing the Cork light vessel, we stopped to ask the skipper's permission to enter harbour. He replied brusquely that the harbour was closed because of the fog, so we made fast alongside to wait it out. The high-pitched shrill of the foghorn quickly proved intolerable as it rattled our brains like peas in a pod. I went aboard the vessel to telephone ashore, leaving the crews holding their ears. The engine-room boys were the exception; they thoroughly enjoyed the situation, because they were the proud possessors of ear plugs. The Duty Staff Officer ashore turned out to be the owner of a charmingly feminine voice. I went into a long flowery description of my marvellous radar and pointed out how easy it would be to enter harbour. The Duty Officer remained unimpressed. She was sorry, but the harbour was closed. After climbing back down to my boat, I found the crew with large wads of absorbent cotton in their ears to keep them from going out of their minds. Blessedly, a message soon came through that we might enter the harbour. We wasted no time speeding away from the light ship into the peace of the harbour.

During the months at Felixstowe more decorations for the 29th had been gazetted. Among the recipients were: Lieutenant C.A. Burk, *491,* two Bars to his DSC, Lieutenant C. Bishop, *464,* DSC and Bar; Lieutenant C.D. Chaffey, *465,* and Lieutenant Keith Scobie, *461,* Mentioned in Despatches; Petty Officer Motor Mechanic Robert E. McGee, *485,* and Leading Seaman Cyril J. French, *486,* Mentioned in Despatches. The citations read as follows: "For gallantry, skill, determination and undaunted devotion during the landing of Allied forces on the coast of Normandy." There were many other officers and members of the crew who were Mentioned in Despatches, but I have just chosen a few at random.

There was little operational work at Felixstowe during the latter part of our stay, for the cold North Sea in winter time was against the Coastal Force. With the going less strenuous, the officers and crews were able to have a good rest. Hal Ritchie rented an attractive little apartment, which soon developed into a club for the 29th under the name of "Chez Ritchie". His little flat was two-storied, and he rented two of the top floor rooms to me for use as a studio. Ronnie Barge and Jasper Cobb, both RNVRs, and I spent our free time dashing off paintings. The light was good, and we spent many relaxing and pleasant hours there. As Hal's comfortable quarters below were often invaded by the men of the 19th, we three painters often helped him with his housecleaning and dishwashing. All the food parcels we received from home were pooled, and we managed to prepare some delicious meals that way. Chuff-Chuff loved the kitchen, and at almost any hour of the day or night we could find him there, revelling in the delights of a Dagwood sandwich. On one of the kitchen shelves were two very large dragon firecrackers, the type normally used for Commando training. Invariably they were contemplated with mischievous eyes. One night as we were all sitting around the grate in the living room enjoying the warmth

MTB 485. Note the six-pounder on the foredeck and the maple leaf badge on the side of the bridge. (PAC PA116486)

of the fire, Chuff-Chuff disappeared to his favourite nook to dream up a little dish for himself. A moment later he came running back with his eyes clamped shut and his hands over his ears. A loud explosion brought us all to our feet thinking that a bomb had dropped. The living room rapidly filled with smoke, and we couldn't see an inch into the kitchen. The temptation had been too great for Chuff-Chuff; he had lit one of the firecrackers and ended the night with a bang.

Once again the flotilla was in a state of confusion because of a change of officers. Barney Marshall had fallen ill with jaundice, and Dick Paddon became CO of *466*. Jessman, Number One of *462*, was posted away, to be replaced by Martin, the Number Two. Robertson left with Jessman, as they were both on loan to the RN for duty in Pacific cruisers. In *486* I had two Red Snoots; Ireland became Number One and Sabiston became my Third Officer. As of 15 January the 29th was to be based at CFMU 1 under Commander Brind, and the time drew near for the flotilla to sail for Ostend.

Glen Creba's love came down for the few remaining days before we sailed, and the flotilla officers met her at the Felix Hotel. She was a tiny, vivacious Canadian Army nurse with beautiful auburn hair, and she was very attractive in her smart uniform. They made a lovely couple, as Glen was a fair, clean-cut young fellow. Both were extremely happy and appeared to be very much in love, and they provided the happy ending to our days at Felixstowe.

The morning of 15 January dawned beautiful and clear, and *486, 491, 462, 485, 464,* and *466* set sail under a cloudless cobalt sky. The boats sped by the Cork light vessel, crews and officers enjoying the bright sunshine, and about half way across the Channel a voice came over the RT: "Hello chicks. Hello chicks. This is Glen calling. I have an important message. Over." All the boats answered Glen in rotation to pass his message. His voice came back over the air, "Hello chicks; this is Glen. Remember that charming little girl you met last evening? Well, we became engaged last night. Over." The flotilla burst into joyous shouts and congratulations flew to *485*, Glen's boat. The excitement was too much for Bobby Moyse, who promptly rammed Daddy Bones's boat. Thereafter, *462* sported a large tingle in remembrance of the happy occasion.

The six craft glided over the smooth, oily sea to the tricky harbour of Ostend, where two sunken wrecks blocked part of the entrance. We gingerly manoeuvred past these obstacles and continued on to the Coastal Force Base, which had once been used by the German 'M' class minesweepers and the E- and R-Boats. Once there, we had to squeeze through a group of 'D' class MTBs into the tiny basin known as "the creek", which was disgustingly oily and muddy. As soon as we had secured everyone raced aboard *485* to shake hands with Glen and give him congratulatory slaps on the back. Then I nipped up to pay my respects to Commander Brind, who was in charge of CFMU 1.

That night *491* and *466* (Daddy Bones and Dick Paddon) were to patrol with a frigate and a destroyer about ten miles northwest of Ostend. As evening drew on the two boats slipped out of harbour, while aboard snugly secured *485* a great celebration party was developing in honour of Glen's engagement.

The festivities weren't too far along when a large truck arrived to drive the officers and their gear to their new billet at the Queen Mary Hotel. God knows what the name of it had been before the liberation; it had been the German E-Boat Officers' Mess. Joseph, the manager, greeted us and showed us to our various handsome rooms. All told, the accommodations were excellent, although there was very little coal in Belgium, so we had only one small stove to keep us warm in the dining hall. Once everyone was settled we had a jolly meal, with wine, and then decided to see the highlights of Ostend.

After visiting many gay clubs we came to the *Cercle Interallié,* where Bobby Moyse went through the revolving door first, followed by Bish, Glen, and myself. No sooner had we all revolved safely through than a gentleman asked, "Pardon, Monsieur; are you a member of dis club?"

Quick-thinking Bobby replied, "Why of course; I'm Les MacLernon." Les was a Commanding Officer in the 65th Flotilla. Bish said that he was Lieutenant Mabee, while Glen Creba claimed to be Kirkpatrick. When it came to be my turn, I couldn't think off-hand of any yet unnamed CO of the 65th, so I said my name was Fitit-Fatit-Satit.

The Frenchman, looking as if he had not heard correctly, asked "Pardon?" and with a straight face I repeated the name. He let us in. We walked up the palatial staircase flanked with potted palms, and reaching the top we entered a large and beautiful room. Decorated with paintings by contemporary Belgian artists, it was modern in its décor. In the centre of the ceiling was a large chandelier, and beneath that lay a circular dance floor, at one end of which a small but excellent orchestra was playing. The pianist, Charlie, was one of the best in Belgium. The flotilla officers became great friends of Charlie's, and for our succeeding visits the table next to the orchestra was always reserved for the 29th. At the end of the room opposite the orchestra was a magnificent, 30-foot long bar, behind which a dignified character by the name of Gustave pontificated. To the left of the entrance stood a huge fireplace filled with burning logs, and glass-topped tables with comfortable chairs in warm colours were scattered about. After we chose our table, Gustave offered us a famous Belgian drink, the base of which was apples steeped in alcohol, and let me tell you, it was strong, burning wonderfully fiercely all the way down. The place was crowded with many sportive characters from Coastal Force, as well as Army types and Nursing Sisters, and it developed into a delightful night for Glen's pre-nuptial celebrations.

Next morning, the 16th, Daddy Bones returned sad and disappointed from the night's patrol. His unit had been vectored onto the enemy, a group of E-Boats trying to break through the patrol line to lay mines on the convoy routes, but unfortunately the frigate vectored Daddy Bones's boats too late. He first saw the enemy 400 yards ahead when the frigate illuminated the E-Boats

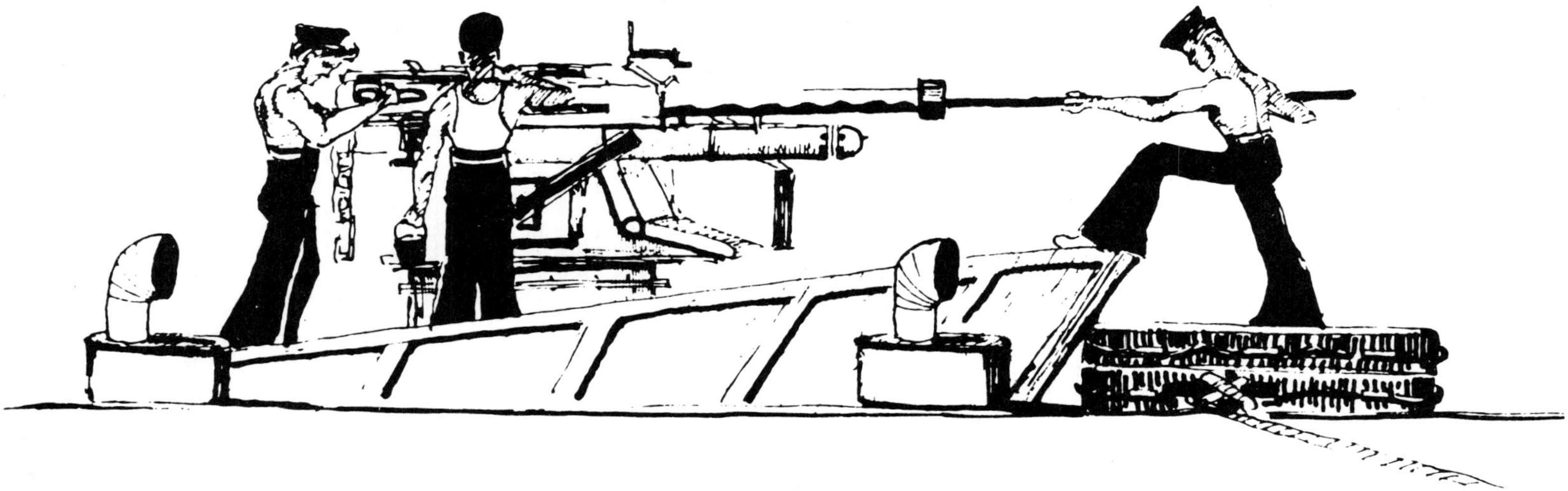

Cleaning the six-pounder. (PAC C127031)

with starshells. *491* and *466* opened fire on the fleeing enemy, which had made smoke and disengaged at top speed with the first starshells; they soon disappeared from sight, headed for home. Dissatisfied, Bones believed he could have done a great deal of damage had he been vectored sooner.

From that time on operations were monotonously quiet. There was the odd chase after the E-Boats, but no real damage was inflicted. The weather was often unsuitable and we would be forced to return to harbour. The boats of the 29th went to sea every night, and at times there was great confusion as we departed in the evening and returned the next morning. Every time we slipped, the colourful little Belgian fishing fleet would be entering harbour, and, trying to wedge by us in the creek, would block the way. The same thing occurred in reverse in the mornings when we returned from patrol, and the whole procedure soon became a frustrating commonplace. To appease us, the fishermen would throw us some of their catch, which landed on our decks, and this was usually accompanied by the shout, "*Voila, la petite Schnellboot!*" We could scarcely blame them for crowding us, because the first man in always got the best price for his fish.

Fishermen were a constant part of the scene at Ostend, as they clopped along in their sabots with salty caps at a jaunty angle. The jerseys of the young fishermen were a brilliant, sharp red, while those of the old fishermen, like their owners, were mellowed by age, sun, and salt. Screaming seagulls hovered over the boats, waiting for their bit as the fish were cleaned, and when anything was thrown overboard they would dive into the water after it, fighting among themselves. The little armada of fishing boats, their warm red sails hanging loosely, drying in the hot sun, were gaily striped with brilliant colours, each in the individual colour-scheme chosen by its owner.

Ostend itself was scarred by five years of war, but in the centre of the square its imposing Gothic cathedral still stood, its two steeples like fingers pointing to heaven. Cluttered about the base of this edifice were small shops and restaurants—Belgium seemed to be a nation of restaurant keepers, for every second building was a café.

The shortage of coal in Belgium was beyond the acute stage. It was a tragedy. The small amount of coal which the Navy required was imported from England. One of my seamen told me the heart-rending story of an old woman carrying a bucket who had asked him for scraps of wood or paper to burn so she might have hot food for her son when he returned from fishing. The seaman, deeply touched, took her bucket and filled it with coal; the poor soul was so overjoyed she tried to embrace the embarrassed sailor.

The flotilla we had replaced had owned a little German Volkswagen, a decrepit contraption which now had four flat tires and was in a generally pitiful condition. Old MacKay and I were looking at it one day, wondering what could be done, and he decided that the best way to start would be to push it over onto the dock near the MTBs. The hood was soon off and dozens of "motor maniacs" set to work on the engine. There was one bald and torn tire which would simply have to be replaced, so I set off hopefully toward the Army Transit Camp. There I met a Canadian Army captain who drove me around all afternoon trying to get a tire, but we could not find anyone who would play. It was nearly 1800 when we decided to try the Army Wreckers (I think that is what they called themselves) and went to the office of the Army Engineer officer. In his broad Scottish accent he promised to see what could be done. He led us out into a jeep graveyard, where we eventually found a reasonably sound-looking tire which the helpful Scottish officer thought would be our best bet. After starting to remove the tire from the jeep, he realized it was his own vehicle, so we selected another tire, this time making sure it wasn't on his jeep. He gave us the complete wheel—rim and tire—and then the Canadian Army officer drove me back to the naval base, where I repaid him with a small smash or two.

Next day our odd-looking car was christened "Little Adolph". It ran like a bomb, and proved to be of great value to us for driving officers back and forth between the Mess and those boats which were slated for sea. One could often see this ridiculous vehicle pulling up in front of the Queen Mary Hotel to debark several officers in various and assorted sea attire, and the line of men climbing out seemed to be neverending. Adolph had become the newest member of the 29th Flotilla. Of the older members, Glen Creba had made arrangements to be married in early March, and Daddy Bones fell ill with jaundice, and much to our regret he had to leave us.

On 30 January more decorations were gazetted, although we didn't receive the news until late in February. Lieutenant C.A. Burk, DSC and Two Bars, was Mentioned in Despatches for the second time, and Petty Officer Motor Mechanic F.A. Walden was also Mentioned in Despatches. The citations read: "For courage and determination in an attack on an enemy convoy while serving in Light Coastal Craft." (This was the action of 1-2 November.)

In the early part of February we received a signal informing us that the Honourable Angus L. Macdonald, Minister of National Defence for Naval Services; Vice Admiral G.C. Jones, the new CNS; Captain Rayner; Mr. John Connolly (later a Senator), who was the Minister's Executive Assistant; and Commander Peter McRitchie would visit the 29th on the following day. Commander Brind and I made arrangements for a sea programme, weather permitting. We also planned a luncheon, and each officer contributed some wine to introduce the pleasant flavour of France.

The following day the visitors arrived by airplane and proceeded directly to the Queen Mary Hotel. The table was elaborately set, and Joseph, the manager, and his helpers were all dressed in sparkling white, for this was a great day for them too. The Minister and the Admiral were introduced to all the officers before the meal began. Then, with the confusion of getting seated, and in true MTB style, I made a bad mistake in etiquette by placing the Minister on my left and the Admiral on my right. After lunch the party left for the dock, where the Minister and the Admiral inspected the crews. (The sea programme had been cancelled as the weather was impossible.) The Minister gave the boats a keen inspection, and later, during an informal chat, I invited him and his party to remain in Ostend for the night so we could show them the night life. He appeared to be greatly touched by the gesture, and would have stayed had the Admiral not had an appointment in London early the next morning.

486's radar was out of order, and although all the brains in Ostend had tried to repair it, their efforts had been to no avail, as the set was completely foreign to them. On 14 February, *486* left for England to have it repaired there. The morning was bright and sunny, but the water was rough, and, standing on the bridge, I was soon soaking wet. After travelling about six miles I decided we had better go back to Ostend, so making a graceful half-circle *486* began to retrace her steps. But after thinking the matter over, I said to the Red Snoot, "What's the use, we've gone this far, and we really can't get any wetter, so we might as well go on to England." Once again *486* altered course and headed in the direction of England. It was a long slog to Felixstowe, and the officers and crew were a miserable, dripping group when they arrived. We were all eager to return to Ostend the following day to rejoin the flotilla.

CHAPTER EIGHT

ALL THINGS COME TO AN END

WE SPENT THE NIGHT IN THE OFFICERS' QUARTERS at Felixstowe, and the next morning, 15 February, I had only just gotten up when Commander Kerr asked me to see him. He took me up to his room, poured out a stiff gin, and handed it to me silently. Senior Officers do not ordinarily offer drinks to their juniors early in the morning, and my heart began to pound in dreadful apprehension. Quietly and without circumlocution, he gave me the painful tidings. At 1630 on 14 February 1945, the 29th Canadian Motor Torpedo Boat Flotilla had been destroyed by fire in the Ostend harbour. His words fell upon me like a sentence of death. I found myself breathing hard, with every muscle in my body taut, and my throat was choked with the horrible hurt.

Commander Kerr went on relating some of the details, but my thoughts were stationary and nothing he said registered. I was living in that inferno at Ostend . . . my lost crews, boats . . . all dying in a red fury of flame. It was some time before I could bring myself to listen to the commander. Fire had broken out, igniting the hundred-octane gasoline and causing the torpedoes to explode. Ostend had been rocked by a series of violent explosions for the space

Opposite: Climbing out of "Adolph" for breakfast at the Queen Mary Hotel. (PAC C127026)
Below and next page. After the disaster at Ostend. (PAC PA116484, PA116485)

AAN HET ZEEWEZEN
464

of seven minutes, and even the shores of England had been shaken by the blast. Seven British and five Canadian MTBs had been destroyed, with the terrible loss of 60 lives. Of these, 26 were members of the 29th Canadian MTB Flotilla, including one officer.

It was the greatest disaster in the history of Coastal Force. The impact of the tragedy rapidly hit the shores, bringing sorrow to all who heard of it, and breaking the hearts of those who had lost their loved ones. From its gallant beginning, the 29th had come to this sad end—from the first action at Dover to the fierce and furious days of Normandy, and thence to Ostend, where, with victory so close at hand, it met its tragic doom.

The Honourable Angus L. Macdonald wrote the following lines of sympathy to the remaining officers and crews of the 29th Flotilla:

> I have been thinking much about you in the last few days, and should like to express my great personal sympathy over what has happened. I know how you must feel about a matter of this kind, but you may be sure that what you have accomplished is, in itself, sufficient to justify you and your officers and men for all time.

To end the story of the 29th Canadian Motor Torpedo Boat Flotilla, whose happy and thrilling moments and sad hours I have tried to recount, I should like to quote this simple poem, written from the heart by Signalman Andrew Cleeland of Lieutenant C.A. Burk's boat:

The raging of the treacherous seas,
Long the arch enemy of the MTBs,
Now ceases to hold us in its spell
As we hear the tale of the Ostend hell.
The truth of cause will be remote,
And intrigue will lend its tragic note;
Here today and gone tomorrow,
As mothers and sweethearts shrink in sorrow;
But above it all is heard the cry—
Oh God, the everlasting question, Why?

The end of it—surrendering E-boats are escorted to England by 'D' class MTBs of the RCN's 57th Flotilla, May 1945. MTB 693 is in the foreground. Photo taken from 745. (RCN R984)

GLOSSARY

Admiral's flag The Admiral's flag denoting his rank was always flown on his flagship or on the barge which he used to move from ship to ship or ship to shore. Whenever the barge passed near a ship or boat, or when a ship passed near the Admiral's flag, the flag would be ceremonially recognized with the appropriate whistle call, or "piped".

Asdic A device used to locate objects (such as submarines) under water by means of supersonic impulses. The name is derived from the acronym for the Anti-Submarine Detection Investigative Committee.

cats The catwalks or temporary walkways running across the decks of a row of boats anchored or moored side by side.

chippie A ship or boat carpenter.

dan-buoy A temporary buoy.

doodlebug German V-1 flying bomb, pilotless and jet-propelled.

drip A reiterated complaint.

E-Boat *Schnellboot,* the German equivalent of the Motor Torpedo Boat.

Gieves Gieves was the supplier of all naval officers' uniforms. The one to which the author refers, the Gieves flotation suit, was a two-piece suit designed to keep one warm at sea.

hard-chine Descriptive of the lower surface of a boat's hull, and meaning that this surface is formed of straight lines rather than rounded contours.

How-How HH, location co-ordinates. In this case, "Negative How-How" indicates that the reported enemy boats are no longer visible on radar.

make and mends The sailors had to clean and mend their own belongings, and time available to devote to such activities was "make and mends".

natter To talk at length on a pet subject.

pipe See "Admiral's flag", above.

pom-pom Single or multi-barrelled automatic gun firing a two-pound shell.

pool ratings Ratings not assigned to any specific crew.

R-Boat *Raumboot,* the German motor minesweeper, the equivalent of the Motor Launch.

rating Any non-commissioned sailor.

rig of the day The items of uniform that were to be worn on specific days or occasions as laid down in orders.

starshell A shell designed to explode in the air and thus illuminate an area.

strakes Continuous lines of protective planking or plates from stem to stern of a boat or ship.

tingle A patch on a boat's hull.

tinsel Small strips of foil dropped by an aircraft to confuse enemy radar.

INDEX

ABBREVIATIONS

AFO	Admiralty Fleet Orders
BP	British Power Boat Company
CB	Confidential Book
CCF	Captain Coastal Force
CFMU	Canadian Flotilla Mobile Unit
C-in-C	Commander-in-Chief
CMB	Coastal Motor Boat
CNMO	Canadian Naval Mission Overseas
CNS	Chief of the Naval Staff
CO	Commanding Officer
DE	Destroyer Escort
DSC	Distinguished Service Cross
DSO	Distinguished Service Order
LCT	Landing Craft, Tank
LST	Landing Ship, Tank
MA/SB	Motor Anti-Submarine Boat
MGB	Motor Gun Boat
ML	Motor Launch
MTB	Motor Torpedo Boat
NOIC	Naval Officer in Charge
NSHQ	Naval Service Headquarters
OBE	Order of the British Empire
P/O	Petty Officer
QH	electronic navigational aid
RCN	Royal Canadian Navy
RCNR	Royal Canadian Navy Reserve
RCNVR	Royal Canadian Navy Volunteer Reserve
RN	Royal Navy
RNR	Royal Navy Reserve
RNVR	Royal Navy Volunteer Reserve
RT	Radio Transmitter
SGB	Steam Gun Boat
W/T	Wireless Transmitter